THE BOY WHO DREAMT THE WORLD

The Daydreamer Chronicles: Book 1

Jethro Punter

To my wife, who put up with me spending countless hours with my head in the clouds, and my children, who encouraged me to put it there in the first place

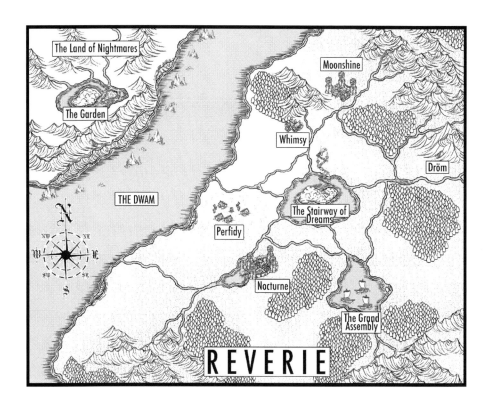

CHAPTER 1

The giant flying creature roared as it caught the breeze with its broad, strong, sinewy wings. Bright green membranes interlaced with darker brown strands. Around it flew its siblings, sharing the same thermals as they circled higher and higher. As the sunlight broke through the clouds it shone through the thinner sections of the creature's wing, giving a gentle green glow and highlighting the slim and long-limbed figure hunched tightly on its back.

"Adam," a voice intruded into the scene. "Adam... are you listening?"

Adam blinked, his view zooming back as the flying beast becomes smaller and smaller, eventually blurring slightly and then refocusing to show it as just another leaf. One of many dancing in the gentle breeze, below the old oak outside the classroom.

Adam was staring out the window and daydreaming, pretty much his favourite past-time but also pretty much the worst thing to be doing in Miss. Grudge's class.

"Adam pay attention please," said Miss. Grudge, her fierce expression at odds with the calm tone of her voice. "Can you perhaps manage to repeat back to me what I just said?"

Pulling his gaze away from the window and the swirling leaves, he turned to face the room. "Um, it was "pay attention please," I think?" Adam replied, his mind still not completely in the present and his instincts for self-preservation apparently not yet fully engaged.

"Oh, very good. Top marks for observation," Miss. Grudge's voice was dripping with so much sarcasm that Adam half expected to find it pooling all around his feet. In his mind it was a bubbling green liquid that would burn through his shoes like acid if it touched them. Without really thinking he leant back in his chair, lifting his feet clear of the floor... which didn't really help his situation.

"But before that I asked the whole class a different question," Miss Grudge continued, "which in the circumstances I feel it only fair to allow you to answer for everyone."

Adam wracked his brain, hoping beyond hope that his subconscious might give him a clue, that a tiny sensible part of his mind might have picked up on the question without the rest of his brain realising, and rush in to rescue him. A few options presented themselves;

1. What is the best way to escape from an angry lion?

2. Who was the inventor of the trampoline?

3. How many completely different numbers can you name in twenty seconds?

As none of these seemed massively likely, Adam decided to ignore his traitorous brain, thinking it might be better to stay silent and see if Miss. Grudge offered any further clues.

"Nothing?" asked Miss. Grudge, arching her eyebrow and pulling absentmindedly on the sleeve of her baggy cardigan, a sure sign to her whole class that trouble was brewing.

"Nothing," she repeated, but this time as a frosty statement rather than a question. "As I thought. Very well Adam, in that case, I will see you after the class."

Adam was pretty sure he heard a collective sigh of relief from the rest of the classroom as they realised that the punishment on this occasion would be restricted purely to him.

After this initial excitement, the rest of the day's classes passed relatively uneventfully, Adam deciding that he would make a special effort to stay focused and resist the urge to stare back out of the window. This was an effort in which he was largely, although unfortunately not entirely, successful.

* * *

At home that evening Adam sat with his mum in their small end-terrace, talking over their respective days as they ate their tea, facing each other over the little wooden table in the kitchen. There was only just enough space to fit both their plates without them hanging off the edge of the table-top, which meant they were also close enough to easily read every expression on the other's face as they chatted.

Trying not to let his guilt show too clearly, Adam glossed quickly over the detention with Miss. Grudge but described in depth the flight of the leaves outside the window. In return, his mum skipped the more boring parts of her day working at the nearby DIY store but explained in some detail her theory that Mr. Rogers, a regular customer, was quite probably an accomplished and infamous robber.

In between bites of soggy pizza, a slice of which she occasionally prodded into the air to emphasize particularly important parts of the story, she told Adam that during the last two weeks Mr. Rogers had bought far too many expensive drill bits, disposable overalls, torches and goggles to be involved in anything as boring as regular household projects. She was grinning broadly as she said all of this, eyes twinkling, particularly when she described Mr. Rogers as 'the Tabby', infamous middle-aged cat burglar, so Adam presumed that the story might not be completely true.

Like Adam, his mum had a friendly, animated face, and her enthusiasm for the day's tales was reflected in her constantly changing expressions. Her eyes would widen as she recounted the more exciting parts, while the corners of her wide mouth twitched with remembered smiles when recalling funny events. Also in common with Adam was her size, no more than five feet tall. Although her personality seemed to be several sizes too big for her body, spilling out at every opportunity and filling the space around her with fun and laughter.

Adam and his mother would regularly pass their evenings this way, with the relatively dull humdrum of their days made more exciting by applying a thick varnish of imagination. Normal events would become epic adventures and otherwise boring people would have extravagant backstories or mysterious hidden agendas to uncover.

As they sat together each night the otherwise limited geography of their lives, dictated by the daily walk to school or work and the small cast of regular daily characters they dealt with, would fade away and be replaced with a world which offered far greater possibilities.

Ever since Adam could remember their life had been like that, with his mum a bottomless source of amazing tales and exciting games. Viewed from the outside their life may have looked very ordinary, boring even, but from the inside looking out the view was far brighter and more interesting.

Recently though, although he hadn't said anything and felt guilty just for thinking it, Adam had started to question the stories and wonder if there wasn't more to life than recounting imaginary adventures.

He couldn't help looking at the cramped kitchen and the mismatched chairs, the old TV and the baggy, tired sofa, and want a little more for them both. He wasn't entirely sure in his own mind what had changed, or was changing, wondering perhaps if it was just as he grew older it was getting a little harder to see past the increasingly real world around him.

Still, despite the nagging feeling he was now getting too old for bedtime stories, Adam happily listened to the tales his mum told him that evening, and when he slept his dreams were once again full of adventure.

* * *

"Hey, Adam, wait up a minute," shouted a friendly voice behind him as he started the walk to school the following day. Adam smiled and turned to greet Charlie Henson, his closest (which also meant most patient) friend. He was, in several respects, the direct opposite of Adam. While Adam was short and compactly built, Charlie was tall for his age and slightly gangly. Adam had wild, mousy hair that was almost impossible to control despite his best efforts, while Charlie had a thick mop of dark brown hair which he constantly experimented with, somehow managing to find styles that seemed to be completely unique to him.

Adam was rarely found without his head somewhere in the clouds, whereas Charlie's open and freckled face contained a brain that was capable of focusing like a laser, able to concentrate intensely on a single thing at any point in time. Despite, or perhaps because of their differences the two had formed a solid friendship ever since they had been seated next to each other in class, back in year two.

Charlie enjoyed the variety of games, schemes, and plans that came out of Adam's fertile imagination and in return, Adam benefited from Charlie's ability to actually get things done. Although there was often still a big gap between the grandeur of Adam's plans and the reality of what they achieved, this was still a hundred times more than Adam would ever have managed on his own, with any number of amazing ideas which would otherwise have never made it out of his head.

"How did it go with Miss. Grudge yesterday?" Charlie asked with a look that was meant to show friendly concern but was equally obvious as a transparent attempt to get the full and gory details, invariably met with over-dramatic gasps of admiration and horror.

Charlie had personally never had a detention, which in Miss. Grudge's class was rare in itself. In addition, as far as Adam was aware, he had never received a bad mark or even a cross word. As a result Charlie only experienced the mysterious terrors of detention through the tales he got from Adam, which Adam generally tried to make a little more interesting than the boring reality.

He sometimes felt that Charlie, with his head packed full of brains, was unlikely to genuinely believe that he had spent an hour being forced to walk circuits of the class whilst reciting facts from Roman history in Latin (which he very obviously could not speak and which they had never been taught), but Charlie seemed to enjoy the tales all the same.

As he finished this week's exciting but transparently false tale, he could tell that Charlie was a little distracted, paying less than his usual rapt attention.

"At least it should be an interesting day at school," Charlie said, obviously unable to contain his own news any further. "I heard my mum and dad saying last night that one of their old friends has moved back into the area and that their daughter will be starting school in our class."

Adam shrugged, new kids in class were unusual but not unheard of, and as a result not really that exciting. Undeterred Charlie continued.

"Their friends apparently have travelled all over the world doing some sort of exciting job, although I am not sure quite what. I bet she has all sorts of interesting stories about their travels."

While this did make things sound a bit more appealing, Adam couldn't help feeling a small pang of jealousy, interesting stories were very much his area, and he wasn't sure about someone new sharing his territory.

Charlie continued to chat excitedly as they made their way down the street and through the school gates, not leaving enough of a gap for Adam to get a word in.

By the time they reached the door of their classroom, Adam was exhausted from all his insincere nodding and smiling.

As they sat in class Adam looked around the room to see if he could spot the new starter, but by the time Miss. Grudge arrived to take the morning register there were still no new faces. Charlie's mood by this point had dropped all the way from massively over-excited down to borderline despondent, but then Adam saw him sit up stiffly in his seat as a small figure quietly followed Miss. Grudge into the class.

"Now class..." said Miss. Grudge "...before we start today, I have the pleasure of introducing a new member of the year group, this is Nora Penworthy."

Standing shyly to one side of Miss. Grudge, Nora was a particularly small girl, smaller even than Adam, who up to that point had enjoyed the dubious privilege of being the shortest one in the class. She had short dark hair, cut into a neat bob, slightly downcast eyes and a mouth that, while it looked like it could manage a good smile, was currently twisted into a nervous grimace. Overall she gave the impression of someone who desperately wanted to be somewhere else, a feeling with which Adam could fully sympathise.

"Right class, who can I rely on to look after Nora? If someone could please volunteer to partner with her for the day," continued Miss. Grudge.

Adam felt the gust of air as Charlie's arm shot up next to him.

"Thank you, Charlie," said Miss. Grudge, then turned to Adam, the sour look on her face deepening. "Adam if you could please find yourself a new desk?"

Adam picked up his books, shot Charlie a quick look meant to express the terrible betrayal and disappointment he now felt and slouched across the class to an empty desk at the rear of the room.

For the remainder of the day, Adam sat in a deep and miserable grump, staring daggers alternately at the back of Charlie and then Nora's heads. Aside from making him feel slightly better, the daggers unfortunately didn't appear to have any other effect, with Charlie and Nora seeming to get on alarmingly well. As the day drew to a close Miss. Grudge handed out the homework assignment for the week.

"Pay attention Class, this week we are starting our project on genealogy. To get us started I would like you all to produce a short presentation on your family tree."

Ignoring the collective sigh from around the room, she signaled the end of the school day, also making it clear that she expected to see some initial progress on the project by the following morning. While Adam piled his textbooks back into his school bag and pulled on his coat, Charlie and Nora leant in towards each other muttering plans for their, no doubt amazing, projects.

"You all right Adam?" asked his mother from the kitchen as Adam trudged through the doorway and grumpily slung his bag on the floor, relieved to be home from school.

"Fine," muttered Adam and slumped heavily down onto the old sofa, destroying the last couple of stubbornly working springs in the process.

"Obviously." His mum rolled her eyes slightly. "Give me a minute. I'll finish making my tea, get you a drink and maybe we can chat about whatever it is that's making you feel 'fine'."

A few minutes later, and following a number of further protestations that he was definitely fine, Adam had admitted the truth to his mum, specifically:

1. A new girl had started in his class;
2. She had immediately stolen his best friend;
3. Charlie was an idiot; and
4. Basically, his life was now over.

His mum smiled sympathetically. "Don't worry," she told him reassuringly, "new people always seem exciting, but you and Charlie have been friends for years. This new girl won't change that. Just give him a bit of time, you'll see."

"But she seems really exciting," Adam replied, aware that he sounded a bit whiny and feeling annoyed at himself... although not quite annoyed enough to stop.

"She's travelled all over the world with her interesting parents doing amazing mysterious jobs. They're probably superspies or international jewel thieves or something. How am I supposed to compare with that?"

For a second his mother looked a little hurt, but then she smiled. "I know that you and Charlie have had all sorts of adventures together, I am sure every bit as exciting as this Nora and her family could ever have imagined. Don't you remember the off-road buggy you built together in his garden?"

Adam could remember all too clearly, it had been a glorious afternoon, charging around a makeshift track, although Charlie's parent's wheelbarrow had sadly not survived its sudden transformation.

"But that's the point, none of our adventures are real," Adam complained, stubbornly refusing to let the happy memory cheer him up. "They're all just silly stories or make-believe, like the buggy. How's that supposed to compete with real life?"

At this his mother's forehead crinkled into the start of a frown, making the soft lines around her eyes, which normally accompanied her smiles, more prominent.

"Don't say that," she said, surprisingly serious for a moment. "You might not realise it now, but all those games, all those stories that you and Charlie have shared, they are the best thing you could ever do."

She caught the look in Adam's eyes. "Honestly," she added, her face relaxing back into its more habitual playful grin, "you would miss them terribly if you ever stopped. Life would be boring... really, really boring."

While in truth he didn't feel much better, Adam decided to make a brave face of it, managing to force a weak smile of his own. It wasn't terribly convincing, looking rather lost and isolated below the rest of his face which remained determinedly miserable, but it was a start.

"Okay," he conceded, although still a little reluctantly. "Anyway, with Charlie and Nora so friendly all of a sudden, I'll need to start work on my homework without him, for the moment at least. We need to do a project on our family tree. Have we got any old family photos or things I could take into school tomorrow?"

"I'm not sure." His mum stopped to think for a moment. "We lost a lot of things like that in the fire, but I'll have a look and see what I can find for the morning."

While they rarely spoke about it, 'the fire' was one of the reasons why Adam and his mum had moved and now lived in their cramped terrace with the mismatched furniture.

Although Adam didn't really remember it, his mum would occasionally talk about their previous home. To listen to her, on the rare occasion when she was in the mood to share her memories, their old house had been wonderful, big family rooms, open fires and a large, sprawling wooded garden close to a river.

A couple of years ago Adam had mentioned it to Charlie, who seemed confused by Adam's explanation, saying that because of things like insurance Adam's mum would have been able to buy another house pretty much the same as the last. But when Adam had rushed home with this good news, rather than being happy his mum had been unusually angry. As a result, Adam hadn't mentioned it since.

That night when he slept, rather than dreaming about the story his mum had told him, as he normally did, Adam dreamt of fire. It was rippling lazily up tall stone walls and wrapping itself lovingly around wooden beams that hung low from the ceiling. The air was full of crackling and popping sounds and in the background two voices were shouting, a higher voice that Adam recognised as his mum's and a deeper one that Adam felt he should know but couldn't place. Then the dream faded and with it came a more comfortable and settled sleep.

* * *

Before he left for school the following morning his mum handed him a large envelope stuffed with printouts of old photos.

"I found a few saved on the computer that I thought you could use," she explained. "I've written the names on for you."

Adam quickly leafed through the photos, his mum's small neat handwriting on each one, covering a few basic details.

The first one had *Uncle Arthur, Australia, born 1942*, under a photo of a tall, friendly-looking man, while his mum had written *Cousin Penelope, Ireland, born 1937, died 2012*, by a black and white image of a stern woman standing in front of a low roofed cottage.

Most of the family, as far as Adam could tell as he flicked between the various images, either lived a very long way away or were no longer alive, but at least it gave him somewhere to start with his project, so he smiled his thanks to his mother as he stopped briefly to grab his packed lunch, before dashing out the front door.

Pulling the envelope back out of his bag, he took another look at the photos as he made his way to school. It seemed like his mum hadn't managed to find any original photographs, with all of the images being photos she must have had stored on her laptop, printed onto a few sheets of paper. But at least he now had five or six family members to refer to, and he started to sketch out the start of how the family tree might look in his head as he walked down the road.

It was a shame that none of them seemed that exciting, he had hoped that the project might uncover a secret connection to someone amazing, like King Arthur, but maybe that would come when he started digging into the project in more detail.

As he turned the last corner before reaching school a gust of cold air caught him by surprise and nearly snatched the bundle of papers from his hand. Gripping them tightly Adam quickly stuffed them back into the envelope, slightly crumpled, and then held it tight to his body to protect it from the suddenly strong wind, before zipping it back into his school bag.

Despite his coat, Adam felt surprisingly cold and turned up his collar to try and get rid of the chill he could feel creeping up his back. Even so, he couldn't shake the feeling of icy fingers on his neck for the rest of his walk.

When he arrived in class Charlie was already in his normal seat and out of habit Adam nearly sat down next to him before remembering that Nora had taken his place. Ignoring Charlie's tentative smile he moodily made his way back to the desk he had used the previous day, right at the other end of the room. However, as the rest of the classroom filled up, the seat next to Charlie remained empty, and following the morning register it was clear that Nora wasn't turning up.

While he was tempted to re-take his normal chair, he was still smarting from being second choice, so Adam stayed in his new seat rather than re-joining his friend and spent the day working on his project alone.

By the end of the afternoon he had managed to get the start of his family tree roughly laid out, with several of the images provided by his mother cut out and stuck onto a larger sheet of paper that now covered most of his desk. Looking across the various family members and then down to the two small photographs of him and his mum at the very bottom, he tried to see any areas of similarity or resemblance, searching for features that reflected his own, but despite his efforts he struggled to find much of a pattern.

The best he could come up with was that they all had faces, and that one or two of those faces looked quite grumpy. This reflected how he was feeling, but he was almost certain that grumpiness wasn't something passed down genetically, and it was very unlikely to get him any points with Miss. Grudge.

❊ ❊ ❊

As he walked home after school Adam turned the day over in his mind, his work in progress on the family tree re-opening a lot of old unanswered questions. Aside from the photos of him and his mum the other images hadn't meant much to him, despite his best efforts.

While some of his classmates had taken pleasure in pointing out various aunts and uncles, grandparents and favorite cousins as they worked on their own projects, until the previous day he hadn't even heard of the family members he was now mapping out.

While he knew that it was going to be a bit of an awkward conversation, he decided that this evening he was once again going to ask his mum to tell him more about his wider family and their life before the move.

Reaching his street Adam felt the same strange cold sensation down his back that had chilled him on the way into school that morning. Pulling his coat tightly around him and looking around he tried to see where the sudden icy breeze was coming from. He also couldn't help noticing that the bushes that ran up the side of the street were completely still, while a random discarded crisp packet was also lying unmoving on the street just ahead of him, seemingly untouched by the gusts of wind that he could feel.

Quickly making his way to the front door Adam pulled out his key, keen to get out of the sudden cold, however as he reached for the door it swung slowly inwards without him needing to unlock it.

Although unusual, his mum had occasionally left the door unlocked in the past, at times when she had to move a lot of shopping from the car to the house, or when she knew that Adam would be home soon, so he wasn't particularly concerned. However, this changed as soon as he made his way into the narrow hallway of the house.

While it was always a bit of a mess, with random shoes, bags, and other knick-knacks generally dumped in piles, requiring you to keep half an eye on your feet as you walked through to make sure you didn't trip, the hallway was almost unrecognisable.

The row of coat hooks where Adam would normally put his jacket and school bag at the end of the day was hanging half off the wall at an awkward angle, nearly catching Adam's head as he stepped forward, momentarily disoriented as he tried to take in all of the unexpected mess and damage around him.

He passed the small table where the house phone and a bowl for keys and loose change were generally placed, but it had been tipped onto its side, and its contents strewn haphazardly across the tiled floor.

He tried to call for his mum but found he wasn't able to manage anything other than a panicked intake of breath. Stopping for a moment, leaning his back heavily against the wall, he tried again, and this time managed something halfway between a squeak and a weak shout.

"Mum, Mum, are you there, are you okay?"

He didn't hear a reply, but he knew that his voice had been so quiet that it was likely she wouldn't have been able to hear him, even from the next room. Calming his breathing down a little and pushing himself back off the wall Adam made his way into the living room, where the wreckage he had seen in the hallway continued.

The old saggy sofa was torn to pieces, the cushions spread across the room, the cheap and itchy stuffing spilling out from wide, ugly looking rips. The television had been tipped onto the floor, shards of broken glass from the shattered screen sticking up from the carpet, crunching under Adam's shoes as he walked back through to the hall.

He called out for his mum again as he made his way up the stairs, the pattern of destruction repeated in the upstairs rooms.

The door to his mother's bedroom hung open, one of the hinges hanging half off the wall and the surround to the other shattered, where the door had been violently knocked loose of its frame.

If the chaos of the rest of the house had been bad, his mum's bedroom was hardly recognisable as a room, looking more like a rubbish tip, with no sense of ever having been lived in or loved. Every cupboard had been emptied randomly across the floor, the wardrobe was tipped onto its side spilling its contents, and every piece of material appeared to have been shredded. Even in his shell-shocked state, Adam wondered what kind of person could do all of this. The amount of damage seemed far beyond that of a simple burglary, there was an underlying sense of anger and violence to the whole thing that sent a cold, heavy ball of fear right to the base of Adam's stomach.

As he stumbled through the room, not concentrating on what he was doing, the inside of his head as chaotic and messy as the wreckage of his home, Adam caught his foot on a tangle of clothes and tripped forward, the wall of the bedroom passing by his face in a blur as he fell. Then he felt a bright flash of pain as the corner of his head caught the edge of the bedframe halfway on its sudden, unplanned journey to the floor.

Adam blinked a couple of times, a mixture of tears and a blurry darkness swimming in from the edge of his vision making it hard to see.

Out the corner of his eye, a bright glinting light cut into the blackness, something under the bed that caught his rapidly diminishing attention. Stretching out his arm, which was starting to feel incredibly heavy, Adam felt his fingers brush against something small and hard wedged into the underside of the bed frame. As his vision faded completely to pitch-black his hand closed tightly around the object, feeling strangely hot in his grasp, and then he dropped away into nothingness.

CHAPTER 2

His head aching, Adam slowly opened his eyes, the brightness of the light making him squint and intensifying the pain he already felt at the back of his head. As his senses slowly returned, vision clearing and the loud rushing noise in his ears fading away to a dull hum, he started to take in his surroundings. He had expected to be in his Mum's room, surrounded by chaotic mess, but as his eyesight cleared and he had the chance to look around, it was clear that this was not the case.

Rather than the view above being a ceiling of any kind, he was looking at an open clear blue sky. The source of the bright light that had stung his eyes was a full and shining sun directly above him, wavering slightly through a thick and muggy heat haze. Turning his head gingerly to the left and feeling the unexpected tickle of grass across his cheek, he could make out more of his immediate surroundings.

He appeared to be in an open clearing, lying directly on a patch of damp grass, with the moisture starting to seep uncomfortably into his clothes. Several metres away he could see a mass of tall plants, swaying gently in the breeze. Although he didn't recognize them, Adam could also now smell an increasingly strong and strange, but not unpleasant, scent which he assumed was coming from the giant yellow flower heads that topped each of the slender stems.

He was also aware of a warm, aching sensation coming from his right hand, which was tightly closed around something, the knuckles of his hand white with the ferocity of his grip. Memories of the last few moments in his mother's room returned and he slowly loosened his fingers, looking down to see what he had found.

There, balanced on his open palm, was a small pendant, silver in colour and attached to a slim chain, currently tangled and wrapped around itself. The tightly coiled chain had imprinted a matching pattern in the skin of his hand, whilst the pendant itself was slightly discoloured with a small cheap looking clasp to one side.

Before he could check any further, he was disturbed by the sound of a polite cough from somewhere behind him. Slowly and a little painfully Adam raised himself up on to his elbows so he could turn to see where it had come from, but as he did so it quickly became clear this had been a very bad idea. The pain in his head that had previously faded returned and worsened as a result of his effort to move, and before he could fully turn around Adam's vision once again began to blur.

"Adam, stay with me, don't fall asleep," came a voice from close behind him. There was a sense of urgency in the speaker's voice, but despite his efforts, Adam couldn't stop himself from slipping back into darkness.

It only seemed moments later when he reopened his eyes, still with the sound of someone saying his name.

"Adam, open your eyes, that's it... good, blink if you can hear me."

Adam blinked, although more to clear his eyes than in response to the request and found himself looking up at the concerned expression of a paramedic leant over him as he lay sprawled back amongst the mess of his Mother's room.

Adam protested rather weakly that he was okay, or at least made a couple of mumbling noises along those lines. But the medic, who turned out to be called Mary and was a cheery (in the circumstances) young Scottish woman, insisted that he was to be helped to the ambulance waiting outside after which he would be driven to the local hospital for a full check over.

"My mum," Adam asked, "where is my mum?" as soon as his head was sufficiently clear to form a more coherent sentence.

Mary didn't quite manage to keep eye contact with Adam as she told him that the first thing to do was make sure he was okay. He had taken a bad bump to the head and there was a chance of concussion, so her priority was to get that looked at. People, lots of professional, dedicated people, were checking on his mum's whereabouts and Mary was sure, she told him, that everything would be sorted out soon.

* * *

But as it turned out, things were not to be 'sorted out soon'. The first few frantic hours stretched out into days, with no news of his mum to reassure Adam as he lay or sat in his hospital bed. He had been told he was being kept in for observation, to make sure that the blow he had taken to his head, now carefully stitched, did not result in any unexpected complications. However as time passed Adam was beginning to think that his head was in fact fine, the ache having fully gone. Rather, he had come to the conclusion that he was now being kept in the hospital ward while a carousel of painfully helpful and sympathetic adults decided what they were going to do with him.

Several of his visitors had been from the police and had questioned him, kindly but thoroughly, about what he could recall about his return home earlier in the week. In return, Adam had asked them increasingly desperately about any progress they had made in finding his Mother.

Unfortunately neither had been able to help the other, with Adam remembering nothing that seemed to be of any help to the police, while they were unable to tell Adam anything useful about his Mum. The only reassurance they could provide was that there was no sign she had been at the house at the time of the break-in.

The days and nights blurred into each other, somehow managing to be both terrifying, with Adam constantly afraid he would hear bad news about his mother, and yet still intensely boring, with long days of doing nothing, waiting for news that failed to arrive. Sleep was always a long time coming, with Adam finding each night dreamless and empty, often waking up feeling more tired than the evening before.

After several more stretched-out days of relentless waiting, he had his first piece of slightly better news when Charlie's parents brought him to visit Adam. His previous jealousy at Charlie's new friendship with Nora was completely forgotten in light of the more serious problems he now faced, and Adam greeted Charlie with delight. He only just stopped short of jumping up and hugging his friend in relief at the sight of a genuinely friendly and familiar face.

While obviously pleased to see him, initially Charlie was still a little awkward, fidgeting with the bag of sweets he had brought Adam and managing to eat at least half of them himself without really noticing.

They started with careful small talk, skirting around the more serious, unspoken things that had happened. The new and hotly awaited superhero film had turned out to be a massive disappointment, school continued to be boring, Miss. Grudge missed Adam terribly (although Adam presumed from Charlie's broad grin that this piece of news might not be completely true), and Nora had not been back in since her first day at school.

The rumour was that she had become very ill almost immediately after joining the class. His previous enmity now completely forgotten, Adam asked with genuine concern what was wrong with her, happy to divert attention away from his own problems. But according to Charlie no one really knew, all he could tell Adam was that she hadn't been seen since her first day.

As their conversation eventually dried up, Charlie's mum ushered Charlie to one side. Mrs. Henson was a short and slightly dumpy woman, free with her good-natured smiles, although Adam knew that she was also capable of being extremely fierce when the mood took her. This was particularly the case when one of Adam and Charlie's less well thought out schemes made a mess of her house, garden or, on one unfortunate occasion, pet Labrador.

While it was a bit unusual and they had needed to make a lot of enquires to get this far, she explained to Adam that, if he agreed, Adam could stay temporarily with them until his mother returned… or until a more permanent solution to his living arrangements needed to be found. She said it in a way that suggested that the second option was only there for completeness, rushing through the words. Everyone knew that Adam's mum would turn up soon and that would be that.

They had been discussing the possibility for the last week behind the scenes, but now they had reached the point where they wanted to see what Adam thought.

As she finished explaining she looked expectantly and slightly nervously at him, her cheeks a bit redder than normal and her fingers fiddling with the hem of her jumper.

For Adam it wasn't a hard decision to make. He had regularly stayed over at Charlie's house, with many of their adventures having been formulated in the treehouse at the bottom of the Henson's garden. Besides which he really wanted to be out of this room, and the chance to stay with his friend was definitely better than the other alternatives he could think of. The only thing that had kept him going was waiting for news of his mother, and he could get that as easily at the Henson's house as anywhere else. Although it still took some time to arrange, by the end of the next week Adam had left the hospital in the Henson's old and battered people carrier.

Finally, after a long day that had ended with a pleasant but slightly awkward meal with the family, Adam started to settle into the Henson's spare bedroom.

The room had previously been occupied by Charlie's older sister, who had since left to go to college and who in Adam's opinion must have had truly terrible taste. The room was wallpapered in a bright and luminous shade of candy-floss pink, which was reflected in the matching sheets and pillowcases on the bed. However, in the circumstances, Adam decided he couldn't be that picky.

He had been given a small suitcase containing a selection of clothes from home, a washbag, and a separate carrier bag that contained all the clothes and belongings that he had with him when the medics had found him. Emptying the bag onto his new bed Adam checked through the sparse contents.

As he moved the crumpled school clothes he had been wearing to one side, Adam noticed that the trousers had a fresh-looking green grass stain down the back and put them in a separate pile to wash. Then, as he picked up his school shirt a small object dropped out from where it had been wrapped, startling Adam for a moment until he realised it was the pendant he had found. He had been so caught up in everything that had happened that he'd completely forgotten about it.

Sitting down on the floor, his back resting against the bed, Adam decided to take a closer look. Unwrapping the chain from where it was tangled about the pendant, Adam let it hang loosely in his hand for a moment, swinging slightly. As before the silver of the pendant appeared to be vaguely discoloured, although the extent and tone of the discolouration seemed to vary depending on how you looked at it. One minute there was a slight greenish tint, the next a gentle glimmer of orange.

Turning his attention to the catch on the side of the pendant he tried to open it, but to his initial surprise and eventual annoyance the catch appeared wedged or possibly rusted in place, and despite several minutes of intense effort he was unable to move it.

Despite his frustration with the jammed clasp, as night drew in Adam was unable to shake the feeling that the pendant was important, or at least that it had been to his mum. So as he finally dropped into sleep, his hand remained tightly closed around it, nestled under his pillow. He found it strangely comforting, as if it somehow brought him nearer to his mother.

CHAPTER 3

"You decided to come back then…"

Adam opened his eyes blearily and rather than the expected sight of the spare room's ghastly wallpaper, he was immediately faced with something, if possible, even more disturbing. A wide grinning face was looking directly down at him, far closer than Adam felt comfortable with.

Brain still fuzzy with sleep, Adam panicked a little and tried to pull his head back, but realised very quickly that he was no longer lying on soft sheets but instead on very hard and stony ground. As a result, the only thing he achieved was a slight but painful bump on the back of his head.

The face, still grinning, if anything more widely as Adam bumped his head, drew back and with his view now unobstructed Adam was able to look more clearly around him. Once again, he appeared to be in a grassy clearing, surrounded by the same tall, swaying plants as before and with the same slightly sweet smell in the air.

"What do you mean, I decided to come back?" Adam stammered, as the figure that had previously been leaning above him moved further back and slowly straightened to a standing position. Adam had been meaning to ask more typical questions for someone waking up in a strange location, such as "where am I?" or "who are you?" or even "why are you so close to my face?", but Adam's mouth had engaged well in advance of his sleep-addled brain.

"I mean exactly that," said the figure, wincing and rubbing its back. "You were here, then you went away… and now you're back."

"And I must say," the stranger added with a slightly more wry version of his previously wide grin, "hopefully for a little longer this time, all this waiting around has given me terribly stiff joints."

Adam studied the man in front of him, or at least he presumed it was a man, as the figure looked quite different to anyone that Adam had ever seen before. In addition to the large round head, the figure's limbs seemed uncomfortably long and spindly, whereas the body was both shorter and broader than Adam would generally have expected.

Still, the clothes looked decidedly masculine, with long pinstriped trousers tapered down to well shined pointed boots, a brightly coloured waistcoat and a short frock coat with a similarly garish lining, which clashed extraordinarily badly with the waistcoat. The whole outfit was finished off with a particularly tall top hat. So for the minute Adam was sticking with his description of the figure as a 'him' of some sort.

As Adam calmed slightly, he returned to the questions he had originally intended to ask.

"Where am I? The last thing I remember was falling asleep."

Then he paused and repeated what he had just said back to himself. "...falling asleep." Relief flooded through him. "Of course, I'm asleep... this is a dream."

"Yes, yes indeed it is," said the figure in front of him, smiling widely once again. "Not just a dream young man, this is THE Dream."

As he emphasised the word 'THE' he stretched out his arms and raised them to either side, as if to encompass all of the surrounding world. "This is Reverie, the great dream, and you young Adam are most welcome here."

"You know my name," said Adam, the more logical questions he had prepared slipping again to the back of his brain, "how do you know my name?"

"How do I know your name?" the figure repeated as he lowered his arms and folded them across his rotund middle. "That is a good question, but there are plenty of others. You might also ask "how did I know you would be here?" or "how did I know you would arrive now?""

"Yes," replied Adam, his brain still fuzzy, struggling to keep pace with all this sudden strangeness. "I mean, if you could answer all of those please?"

"I will answer all your questions as we walk," said the odd figure, leaning down and offering Adam a slender and long-fingered hand. "But before we go any further, as I currently have the advantage of knowing your name, I will share mine with you."

He paused, struck what Adam thought was an overly dramatic pose and said, "You may call me Lucid."

Adam looked back blankly. "Okay, um ... Hi Lucid, pleased to meet you," adding in the privacy of his head, "even if you are just a weird figment of my imagination."

It was immediately clear that Lucid had been expecting a rather bigger reaction than Adam had provided. His eyes narrowed and there was a pale, but noticeable, reddish flush starting to develop on his round cheeks. Adam quickly wracked his brains, trying to think of any reason why the name should mean anything to him, and what reaction Lucid had been expecting.

Perhaps he should have said, "Hooray it's Lucid!" or should it have been, "oh no... not Lucid, please let it be anyone but the infamous and terrible Lucid." But neither meant anything to him. Nor did any of the many varied options in between these two extremes. To Adam it was just a nonsense name.

Exhaling an aggrieved sounding, "Hmmpf" Lucid, obviously still not happy with Adam's reaction, turned sharply on his heel. "Come along or we shall be late." With that he began to stride away, the unusual length of his legs taking him several metres from Adam in a matter of seconds.

"Wait," said Adam, scrambling to his feet. "Late for what? I don't even know where I am, let alone what I could be late for."

He began to follow the rapidly receding figure, although he was not quite clear why he should do so. "After all," he thought to himself, "it's my dream."

While he stumbled along trying to catch up, at the back of his mind he also wondered why he was letting some odd-looking dandy in strange clothes boss him about. Despite this he didn't stop, but rather continued after the increasingly distant Lucid. Dream or not, things were far too strange and interesting to leave as they were.

"Wait!" he shouted again as he drew closer, "you said you would answer my questions while we walk."

Lucid paused mid-stride and allowed Adam to catch up with him.

"I did," he conceded, "and so I shall, ask away and I will do my best to furnish you with answers." With that, he started to walk again, although slightly more slowly than before.

Deciding to ignore the stern expression which remained on Lucid's face, Adam asked him, "So how do you know my name, really?"

Lucid half turned to him as they continued to walk and favoured Adam with a gentler look, although his smile had not yet returned.

"Your mother told me, she also told me where you would appear in our world." He thought for a moment. "More specifically she said that I should wait for you in the fields outside the City where you eventually awoke."

"Unfortunately," he added, "although I was told you were due to arrive soon, she did not inform me exactly when. So I have been seated on a variety of very uncomfortable logs and rocks in that accursed field for the best part of a week, day and night."

This statement seemed to bring back some unpleasant memories for Lucid, who rolled his shoulders back with a slight groan.

"Every time I would swear that the following day I would bring a seat or a cushion, and every day I didn't bother, convinced it would be the last before you arrived, a decision which I am sadly still paying for."

But as Lucid continued to moan about the state of his back, and probably most of the rest of his anatomy, Adam had stopped paying attention, his previous train of thought completely derailed by the references to his mother.

"You know my mother?" he asked, "how, how do you know my mother?"

"Simple," replied Lucid, "she used to visit me often when she came here, many times she and I would chat as we walked this same route between the fields and the City."

"She came here?"

"Yes indeed," Lucid gave a slight nod, appearing to enjoy the chance to speak of the matter. "Just like you, whenever she visited. she would appear in that grassy area in the middle of the trees, I have no idea why, but it appears to be a special place in that respect." Lucid paused for a moment and smiled again, caught up in pleasant recollection.

"The first time she caught me quite by surprise. Long before I joined the Five. I was just taking a stroll, clearing my head away from the hubbub of the City and nearly tripped right over her. She was a silly girl back then, your sort of age most likely and quite unaware of what she had achieved. She was convinced that nothing here was real and therefore quite unconcerned, at least to begin with, about the consequences of her actions."

Lucid stepped up the pace as his reminiscing continued, and Adam noticed the grass track they had been following slowly giving way to a more substantial stone footpath. It was still rather overgrown and unkempt, but a definite sign that they were on a path to somewhere.

"Still, all that changed over time," Lucid continued, "eventually she accepted what she was and became the great woman you must know."

Adam didn't immediately answer and remained a few paces behind as he gathered his thoughts. Of course, he knew his mother was a great woman, but in his mind it was a very... normal sort of greatness. She was certainly kind and thoughtful, and on top of that she told great stories, looking at the world through a lens of imagination and wonder, always encouraging Adam to do the same.

But it seemed to Adam that Lucid was suggesting something more than that, some grander and more substantial meaning of 'great'.

"What exactly do you mean," Adam asked, "when you say she accepted what she was?"

"She was something special in this world," said Lucid, "she was a Daydreamer."

Then he turned his head away before Adam had the chance to raise any further questions.

"Come now Adam, we must pick up our pace again, and much as I enjoy the chance to speak of your mother, the rest of that particular story must wait. We are drawing closer to the City and there are three matters I absolutely must discuss with you before we arrive."

Lucid pointed toward the horizon and Adam could dimly make out the edge of what looked to be a sizeable settlement, bounded by high walls. Their elevated position allowed him to see the concentrated mass of houses contained within the walls stretching off into the distance.

"Firstly, whilst I said I found your Mother by accident, which is completely true and exactly as it happened," said Lucid, "it is no accident that she found me. My grandmother, my father, most of my family going back for generations, are Guides. On the incredibly rare occasion that someone crosses over between your world and ours, and does so consciously, then a Guide is there to greet them. Sometimes this is by chance, sometimes by design, but always to introduce them to the world and occasionally, although very rarely, to ensure that they do no harm." Lucid stopped his explanation for a moment, as they walked up a steeper section of the path, saving his breath and energy for the walk.

Catching his toe and stumbling slightly, Adam looked down at his feet as he too started up the slope. While steeper, the footpath underneath Adam's feet was now solid, closely fitted stone. Various irregularly shaped blocks of slightly differing colours were snugly placed without visible gaps despite their irregularity, reminding Adam of a huge, continuous game of Tetris. As this thought passed quickly through his mind, for the briefest moment Adam thought he saw one of the stone blocks right on the edge of his peripheral vision move slightly, but when he turned his head to focus on it, the block was completely and stubbornly still.

"Secondly," Lucid continued, as they reached the brow of the hill and started down the long and gradual walk towards the City, "your mother told me that something bad had come from our world into yours and that here you would, at least for a time, be safer."

Adam thought back to the ransacked house, the smashed chairs and tables, the ripped pictures and the broken belongings. Something bad had indeed come, something bad had taken his home away.

"I believe that this is the reason that you were to be sent here, to find safety, a calm harbour away from whatever your mother was afraid of."

Adam stayed silent for the rest of the walk to the edge of the City, turning the news he had received over and over in his mind. By this point, his earlier and more reassuring thought that he was in a dream seemed less important than it had previously and instead he felt an overwhelming need to find out more. More than anything else the mention of his mother, odd as it was, was something he couldn't ignore.

"If this is a dream," Adam thought to himself as they approached a large set of gates set into the imposing walls, "whether or not it is real or just in my head, I think I would rather not wake up quite yet."

As they passed through the gates, Lucid nodding amicably to the large man standing to one side as they entered, Adam looked around and took in the sights.

"Welcome to Nocturne, greatest City of Reverie," Lucid told him.

The surrounding architecture was an odd mix of the completely familiar and the utterly strange. As they had approached the City from the surrounding fields, all he had been able to see were the tall gleaming white walls and the occasional slim tower rising high above them, thrusting up from between the mass of housing and giving the whole place a slightly fairy-tale look. But now, passing through the gates and seeing the City up close and at ground level, everything looked far more real, more familiar and if Adam was honest, also a little bit grubby.

"So this is the 'Great Dream'?" Adam asked, looking around at the rough cobbles and stained walls.

Lucid looked back over his shoulder, one eyebrow raised quizzically. "What were you expecting, Goblins busily mixing dream potions and giant floating unicorns?"

"No... of course not... I mean, well... perhaps a bit," Adam admitted.

"Sorry, but that's not how this place works. We all just try our best to work around people from your world when you decide to drop by... dreaming or otherwise. Keep your eyes open and you'll see what I mean."

The route they were walking was obviously a main thoroughfare into the City, with a broad road flanked by tall houses with upper stories that leant into the street. Occasionally one of the ground floors would give way to a small shopfront or café, with chairs and tables set into the wide pavements.

Looking more closely at the patrons of the various cafés Adam could see a number that looked very similar to Lucid, talking and drinking with their long limbs stretched out in front of them. Others seemed indistinguishable from the people he recognised from home, although with clothes and hairstyles that he had never seen before, while a third group were much shorter with their faces almost completely covered with thick bushy hair. What looked from a distance to just be a substantial beard, at closer observation proved to be a full face of hair, with only their eyes showing between the bushy growth. All three groups mingled in the cafés or walked down the wide paved streets, chatting easily between themselves in the morning sun.

Suddenly Lucid drew to a halt and grabbed hold of Adam's

arm arresting his movement.

"What is it?" Adam asked him, slightly alarmed.

"Nothing to worry about," replied Lucid "we just need to wait for a moment."

They had reached a crossroads and on either side groups of people had paused their daily activities in the same way as Lucid and Adam, a sense of slight expectation in the air. Adam obediently stood still and looked around to see what the fuss was about. For a minute he couldn't see anything unusual, then from his left a slowly walking figure emerged. It was a short, pretty woman, wearing over-sized pajamas in a cow print pattern. Seemingly completely out of place, she made her way from left to right across the crossroads, apparently unaware of the quiet and respectful groups of people gathered at the edges of the street. It took several minutes for the woman to fully pass them, and looking to his right, Adam could see groups of people further down the street dispersing to make way for her as she continued her slow, measured walk.

"What was that about?" asked Adam, confused by what he had just seen.

"She is a Sleepwalker," replied Lucid.

Adam struggled to prevent a disbelieving laugh slipping out as Lucid continued.

"She is one of those people that has a closer link to this world than most. She, and others like her, can exist in both this world and yours at the same time."

The crowds of people started to thin, allowing them to continue their walk while Lucid carried on with his explanation.

"As I said when you arrived, this is the Reverie, the great dream. Where we stand, where we walk, this is the dream to your waking world, but no less real for all that. Most people from your world come here quite regularly, whenever they dream but they never realise where they are or understand what this all means."

He stopped for a moment, pointing in the direction of the slowly departing woman.

"Then there are Sleepwalkers, like the woman we just saw, who visit here without needing to use the avenue of a dream, some even maintain some limited control over their actions."

Adam nodded, as if he had any genuine idea what Lucid was talking about.

Lucid turned to Adam. "You remember that I said I had three things I had to tell you on our walk?"

Adam nodded again, although in truth he had forgotten, distracted by all the weirdness.

"The third is that above and beyond your Sleepwalkers, you have the true exceptions, Daydreamers like your mother who come here fully aware of their surroundings and who are capable of effecting the world around them, incredibly rare people... people like you."

As Adam struggled to take in all he had just heard, the street that had previously loomed above and around them opened into a wide market square, filled with noise and the bustle of traders, hawkers, and peddlers of all types.

The marketplace was packed densely with a gaggle of people of different sizes and shapes. Cries of market traders carried across the square, competing vigorously to be the loudest and most ear-catching as they advertised their wares. A stall simply called 'bottles and potions' to Adam's right was doing a roaring trade in exactly that, whilst on the other side of the square, a tall cloaked figure was selling improbable looking snacks from a colourful but rather rickety handcart. A small boy handed across a handful of coins and in return received something that in Adam's view closely resembled ghostly candy floss, gently swirling and changing shape in the boy's hands as he nibbled at it.

Adam was pulled left and right by tempting sounds, smells and sights, each one more unusual and fascinating than the last, a pleasing distraction from the confusion he felt. While Adam bounced around between stalls like a human pachinko ball, Lucid patiently tagged along behind, experienced poise letting him cut through the crowds with far more success despite his slightly awkward frame. Then, just as he was approaching one of the more interesting looking food stalls, although not quite sure how, or even if, he was capable of paying for anything, Adam heard a strange noise behind him.

As he turned, he saw a young boy similar in age to his own running madly across the market square, head down and arms pumping determinedly. Then he saw the source of the strange noise he had heard. A little way behind the boy but obviously gaining was a large lion. In fact, as it drew close, he could see that the lion was beyond large, much bigger than any he had ever seen on school trips to zoos or even on any of the nature programmes he'd watched on TV. Something else aside from the sheer size also didn't seem quite right. If you looked closely you could see the lion's feet weren't touching the ground as it ran, rather it was flowing just above the surface of the ground and flickering from move to move like a cheap animation, jumping between frames.

It was also clear to Adam that the boy wasn't going to escape, he was running wildly, without genuine direction, obviously terrified and seemingly completely unaware of the wider audience watching the chase. As the running boy's panic increased further it seemed to Adam that the Lion thing was getting even bigger, its movements more ragged as it drew closer to its prey, its expression more hungry.

"Isn't someone going to do something to help him?" Adam asked, pointing at the boy.

"Bah, it's just a Nightmare," replied Lucid, "not even a good one, more of a slight scare, a bit of a fright maybe." His expression remained completely calm and reflected none of the concern that Adam felt. "Besides the boy is in absolutely no danger, watch...."

Despite the dismissive tone in Lucid's voice and the same apparent lack of concern in any of the other surrounding people, Adam couldn't stop the feeling of rising panic in his own chest.

"But it's almost caught him." He paused and took a deep breath "...besides, from where I'm looking it's not a bit of a fright, it's a massive, horrible monster!"

Pushing forward across the square Adam tried to force his way towards the boy and the pursuing monster, with no real thought in his mind as to what he was going to do next. Shout at the boy, perhaps shout at the lion or maybe throw something to distract it or to get its attention. Although he was not sure what he could do once he had achieved that, other than perhaps get eaten.

He tried shouting, waving his hands and drawing attention to himself, but other than a couple of tuts from bystanders he got no reaction, and neither the boy nor the lion paid him any attention at all. This just left throwing things. He looked around and quickly realised how limited his options were. Essentially, he was left with the choice of hurling a small pebble, something from a nearby food stand or, at a push, his own shoe.

Then something totally unexpected happened. As the creature caught up with the boy and reared up above him, rather than cowering in fear, the look of terror on the boy's face faded completely and was replaced by complete disinterest. His eyes shut peacefully even as the lion's gaping mouth began to close over his head. Then his body dropped to the ground, totally relaxed and unmoving... and with his head completely and very surprisingly still firmly attached.

The lion thing stopped, a look of confusion on its face which would have been comical on something less awful, and began to sniff the air, apparently completely unaware of the boy now lying just below it. Then it raised its head, gave a most unlion like howl and began to fade, or rather to dissipate, coming to pieces and drifting away in the breeze like fragments rising from a paper fire, each burning out and disappearing completely before travelling too far. Below him the boy also began to fade, and after a few seconds nothing was left but a faint and peculiar smell which lingered for a moment. Then that too was gone.

Adam turned to Lucid, who was looking comfortably smug a few steps behind.

"What... what just happened?" he asked, utterly confused.

While it didn't initially seem as if it was physically possible without actually splitting his face completely in two, Lucid's grin somehow got even wider.

"As *nearly* everyone knows," he said, emphasising the word "nearly" more than Adam felt was really necessary, "it's impossible to die in a dream, no matter how bad the nightmare, no matter how dire and dangerous the situation, how very perilous the peril."

He turned to question Adam directly.

"Think of your own nightmares, you always wake up in the final seconds relieved to find out it was all a bad dream, am I right?"

"I suppose," Adam admitted, nodding slowly and thinking back to the worst dreams he could remember and the relief he felt when he awoke, safe in his bed.

"So just think of your world and our world as two sides of the same coin," continued Lucid, rummaging in one of the many interior pockets of his short frock coat and pulling out a small copper coloured coin. "Your world," pointing to one side, "and ours," flipping the coin to its other side. "In one world you are awake, whilst in the other you sleep."

He started to spin the coin between his fingers, showing a dexterity with his hands that contradicted the apparent awkwardness of the rest of his body. "You come to this world when you fall asleep in yours and when you sleep in this world you awake back there."

As he spoke the coin span between his fingers faster and faster, the engraving on each side beginning to blur into a single undefined image. "When the nightmares come you fall asleep here to escape them and awake back home."

"So what happened to that... thing when the boy fell asleep?" Adam asked, still hugely confused.

Lucid stopped for a moment to consider the question. "The shape of the Nightmare was his personal creation, when he fell asleep here there was nothing left to tie it to him, so it left. It lost both its form and its purpose and so went back to where all the Nightmares come from."

"And that is...?" asked Adam, increasingly intrigued.

But Lucid turned away slightly and replied in a lowered voice, the previous lightly mocking tone gone. "I think that's probably enough for now."

Although Adam was still brimming with unanswered questions, Lucid refused to be drawn any further as they continued their journey across the City. Several times Adam had to step aside as some poor soul was pursued down the street by their own personal Nightmare, a young man running from a giggling dentist, a small girl being chased by a clown with a worryingly large head, and most oddly a desperately sprinting middle-aged man being pursued by a giant carrot, which was pogoing madly down the street after him. That one even caught Lucid's attention for a moment, who stopped and applauded the man for his originality.

As they walked Adam also noticed the gradual change in their surroundings. The denser and more worn houses in the side roads that bordered the Market Place with their crooked walls leaning in towards each other, almost touching at the tip of the gable ends, started to give way to wider streets with neatly trimmed hedges and gleaming white-washed walls.

In the distance, one building stood out to Adam, taller than its surroundings and rather out of place amongst the brighter and more regimented houses. To Adam's mind it looked like a mansion from the old TV programmes his mother liked to watch, filled with lovable families of misfit monsters.

The building itself was a patchwork of gothic spires and crooked angles set back behind a high and rusted iron-railed fence. As they turned off the main walkway and started down the footpath through the house's grounds, Adam weaved his way between overgrown bushes and trees that snagged his jumper and snarled his feet despite his best efforts to avoid them, almost as if they were deliberately reaching out for him. Several times Adam turned around when he felt a tug at his sleeve or a pull at his ankle, only to see nothing when he turned, with the feeling that the innocent looking weed or the apparently harmless shrub he had just passed had only stopped moving the second before.

After a few minutes of this, he and Lucid reached a high imposing doorway, solid and ancient-looking wood banded with ornate ironwork. Halfway up the huge door was a large hatch, located at about head height, although currently closed, and immediately to the left a discoloured brass bell hanging from the wall. Without pausing Lucid leant forward and violently shook the chain inside the bell, resulting in a loud and unpleasantly discordant clanging. A moment later there was a clattering sound and a second smaller hatch, which Adam hadn't previously noticed, opened. This hatch was located well below the first, not much more than three feet from the ground.

"Yes?" boomed a deep and menacing voice, "speak your purpose and enter".

Lucid sighed, turned to Adam pulling a rude face, and replied, "I come to speak to the gathering of the Five."

"Your name?" the voice rumbled, even more deeply.

"It's me, Lucid as you well know... oh for goodness sake, do we have to do this every single time I visit?"

"It's the rules," the disembodied voice boomed back, although now sounding slightly less booming than before and rather more peevish. "Do the rest, and properly please."

"Fine," Lucid sighed again, and continued in a sing-song voice, "It is Lucid, third of the Five, greeter and guide."

"Very well third of the Five, you may enter," replied the voice, although you could sense that its heart was no longer in it. There was a brief pause, after which the sound of several loud clanks and bangs could be heard at various heights behind the door, interspersed with muttered grumblings and cursing. This was followed by one especially loud bang and a muffled scream of, "arrrgh, my finger, blasted, stupid door."

With an ominous creak the door then swung slowly inward and Adam blinked a couple of times, his eyes becoming accustomed to the darkness within. He made out a squat figure in heavy-looking robes, although he failed to see any detail beyond that general perception in the dark.

"Come in then," the figure grunted, in the same deep and resonant tones, "I haven't got all day."

"Nice to see you again too," said Lucid, as he strode into the house with Adam following close behind. They took two further steps passing the small, cloaked figure and then the door slammed shut behind them.

CHAPTER 4

"Come on then, don't just stand there like a useless, gormless lump," grumbled the figure as it bustled impatiently past Lucid at approximately waist height.

"Don't worry," said Lucid, with a sideways glance to Adam. "He doesn't mean you. He always greets me in such a friendly fashion, miserable little grouch that he is."

"I can still hear you," the shrouded figure replied as it reached across and lit a lantern hanging from the wall, "besides which, I haven't yet had the time to form an opinion of your new idiot of a sidekick."

As the light bloomed, pushing back the shadows that had previously restricted Adam's view, he was able to properly see their host. The growing light showed the figure to be one of the small humanoids that Adam had passed on the way to the market, the face bushy with hair. In this case the facial hair was particularly thick and streaked throughout with grey, which Adam assumed to be a sign of age. Aside from that Adam got the impression of small, deep-set and sharp looking eyes, a heavy hooked nose and what appeared to be a series of deep scars running across the upper half of his head.

"Have a good stare, why don't you boy," he snapped. "You should have some respect for your elders rather than standing there gawping like a new-born calf."

"Relax Grimble," said Lucid, making a calming motion with his hands, "the boy is new to Nocturne, indeed to the whole of the great dream, so we are all a bit unusual to his eyes. Let me make the necessary introductions, Grimble meet Adam, visitor to Reverie and son of a good friend."

He turned to Adam, "Adam this is Grimble, oldest, grouchiest, and in his own mind at least, wisest of the Five."

"Come along," muttered Grimble, still impatient but appearing slightly mollified by Lucid's words, "the others are waiting in the dining room."

They continued along the passageway, passing a number of large archways capped with stone on their route, each leading to further similarly expansive corridors. The inside of the house, or possibly mansion, (Adam wasn't entirely clear what the cut-off between the two descriptions would be), appeared to stretch off into the distance to a far greater extent than the outside had suggested was possible. Out the corner of his eye he caught Grimble giving him a sly grin, seemingly aware of his confusion.

"Impressive isn't it," he told Adam, "If you weren't with me, I doubt you would even find your way to the bathroom in this place... and if you did it is very unlikely that you would ever find your way back again."

As he said this, he took a sharp turn through one of the archways into a corridor differentiated from the rest by the series of portraits running down the left-hand side. On closer inspection the paintings showed a variety of groups stood in slightly awkward poses, each made up of a mix of the various inhabitants of Reverie he has seen so far, along with the occasional even more unusual looking addition. It was also clear after viewing a few of the pictures that each group consisted of exactly five individuals.

As Adam walked along the corridor, now lingering a short way behind the other two, it seemed that the pictures were arranged in some sort of date order, with a slight change in fashions apparent as you moved along them. Below each picture was a plaque, with five names engraved upon each, although Adam noted that on some plaques one or more of the names had been scratched out or struck through with a thick black line.

Looking from left to right it also appeared that some individuals had been included in more than one picture while the surrounding cast of characters changed around them. As they reached the end of the corridor, Lucid and Grimble stopping at a particularly imposing-looking doorway, Adam could see that the name 'Grimble' was inscribed on the plaques below the last three paintings he passed. In the first and left-hand most image Grimble seemed almost unrecognisable, with thick black hair rather than streaky grey and no sign of the heavy scarring that now marked his face. In contrast, the final picture showed him stood grumpily alongside the elongated limbs of an extravagantly tailored Lucid, his simple robes in direct contrast to Lucid's garish frockcoat, top hat, and striped trousers.

Before Adam had the chance to look too closely at the rest of the individuals on these final portraits Lucid called him across.

"Now Adam, we are about to enter a very important place, so I must request…"

"Insist," interjected Grimble with a glare.

"No… request," continued Lucid calmly, "that you do not speak unless specifically asked to do so. I am sure that you will have many questions and I will answer as best I can after the meeting, but until then I would ask for your understanding and patience."

With that he knocked at the door, although this seemed a bit pointless, as before there was any sort of answer Grimble ducked impatiently under his arm, pushing the door open, and the three of them walked through.

The room Adam had entered was every bit as grand as the doorway had suggested, reminding him of the extravagant drawing or dining rooms he had seen when he had visited a local Stately Home with his school. Heavy curtains covered the windows on one side of the room, a good fifteen feet from top to bottom and currently drawn closed, while a series of large candelabras hung in sequence down the middle of the room. The central and largest of these was hanging directly over a long dark wooden table.

"If you could wait over there please?" Lucid asked, pointing to a small chair against the wall, just to one side of the main gathering.

As Adam made his way over, he got a closer look at the two figures already at the table. The first, seated to one side, was a bespectacled and studious-looking man. Nothing really stood out to Adam as exceptional or unusual about him. He was middle-aged, balding, wearing a tired looking three-piece suit, and wouldn't have looked out of place in the small bank back in Adam's hometown. He also looked like he hadn't slept properly in some time, with every part of him, from his clothes to his face, looking slightly crumpled.

What was left of his hair was similarly unkempt, sticking out at odd angles as it reached the top of his head, as if it had made a determined attempt to get that far and then given up, exhausted by its efforts.

The figure seated at the head of the table was the complete contrast. If the man had been completely bland, perhaps even boring looking, she was about as far from 'normal' as it was possible to be. Every time Adam tried to focus on her his eyes started to water slightly. He got the impression of a young woman with a strange but palpable feeling of warmth and kindness emanating from her in waves. But when he looked directly at her all he could make out was a pale yellow glow in the general shape of a person, blurred and wavering in outline, no detail visible other than two light blue eyes which focused on Adam for a moment before turning back to the table.

"Welcome friends," she began, settling her gaze on each of the others as they took their places around the table, "although we are missing one of the Five today. Maya cannot be with us, as she is still away from the City." As with her appearance, Adam found it challenging to keep track of her voice, one second it sounded young and high, carefree in tone, the next wise and cracked with age.

"Has she sent any news?" asked the bespectacled man, leaning forward slightly. "I am hearing new rumours every day that there is a new Horror forming on the outskirts of Reverie, but no one really knows how big it has grown or where it is headed."

"Nothing yet Henry," replied the woman, "but be patient, she has a great distance to travel and I am sure that we will hear from her soon enough."

"Still," muttered Grimble, half under his breath, "it's not like her to be late."

Lucid, seated opposite him, nodded slightly, Grimble's look of concern reflected more obviously on his expressive face.

"Regardless," the man now identified as Henry continued as he leant forward, the light from the candelabra reflecting brightly off his spectacles, "if the rumours I hear are even partly true then the extent of the Horror is growing slowly day by day."

There was a brief pause in the conversation, the expressions on the participants faces pensive and drawn. Even from his position across the room, Adam could feel the tension around the table growing.

"So what do we do, I'm not for sitting on my hands waiting here," Grimble said, breaking the silence and rising to his feet. "If we don't hear from Maya soon, I say we travel to the outskirts ourselves and work out just what we are facing. We have been here before, as you all know, and we can't afford to repeat the mistakes made in the past."

The glowing woman raised her hand gently. "Be calm my old friend, Maya will return and then we can plan our next move, until then Henry can return to the library and continue to do his job."

Grimble gave an audibly exasperated sigh and returned to his seat, obviously not satisfied with the answer but seeming to be unwilling to argue his point further. Several times Adam also saw Lucid lean forward, as if ready to make a comment, but on each occasion someone else would take the discussion in a different direction and he would sit back again without speaking. For someone so assured in his regular conversation, he seemed surprisingly overawed by the rest of those seated around the table, far meeker than Adam would have expected.

The meeting continued late into the evening, with a great deal of talk, although to Adam's untrained ears there appeared to be little progress made or agreement reached.

More than anything it made him think of the Mad Hatters tea party, but one in a strange alternate universe in which Alice was made of glowing light, the rabbit was incredibly grumpy, and the main topic of conversation was apparently the end of the world.

Eventually, one by one, the figures around the table stood, made their apologies and left. First to go was Henry, who nodded to Adam with a tired half-smile as he passed, pausing briefly to put on a tatty bowler hat and scarf before leaving the room. Shortly after Lucid stood and made his way over to Adam, leaving Grimble and the strange woman still deep in animated conversation.

"Come along then," said Lucid, gesturing to the door. Adam stood, yawning and stretching his arms as they made their way back into the portrait corridor.

"What was all that about?" asked Adam. Despite his tiredness he could hardly wait for the door to swing closed behind them before beginning with his questions.

Lucid turned to him with a weary expression, "I remember my promise to answer your questions Adam, so I will do my best... ask away."

"Firstly, who are you all?" asked Adam. "Who is that Maya you were talking about and who was that... woman at the head of the table?"

"As a group, as you probably gathered," Lucid began, "we are known as the Five."

His high forehead creased as he continued. "It's perhaps not an original name," Lucid admitted, "but one which is extremely accurate in its description. Ours is not a particularly unruly world, with little need for policing, so for as long as most can remember there has been a small group of just five individuals responsible for keeping things in Reverie stable and safe. These days most think we are an archaic, unnecessary throwback to more un-enlightened times, but..."

He stopped mid-sentence, changing topic.

"With regards to the individuals you ask about, Maya is the simpler explanation. Each of the Five has a set job to carry out, most suited to our natural gifts or talents. Maya is particularly good at scouting and so she had been sent to investigate rumours about the forming of a new Horror and report back. However, she should have been in touch by now and we have heard nothing, which is... unusual for her."

"But," he added, appearing to mentally shake himself clear of an unpleasant avenue of thought, "I am sure she will return soon, she is exceptionally good at her job."

"The second half of your question," he continued, "is harder to address. The head of the table was taken today by someone we call the Lady. She is, as far as we know, one of a kind. Very rarely, almost as extraordinary as the arrival of a Horror, is the creation of something in many ways the opposite, a being made up of pure dreams."

Adam thought back to the strange glowing figure and the difficulty he had in trying to make out her features.

"Someone, somewhere had such an incredibly powerful and resonant dream that its energy continued to exist after they awoke. On the amazingly rare occasion that takes place then a being such as the Lady can come into being. Each of them is entirely different from the previous one and leads a very strange existence as the only one of their kind. No one knows how long each being dreamed into existence will last before finally disappearing. Sometimes days, sometimes, as in the case of the Lady, for several or even tens of years."

"It sounds kind of..." began Adam, trying to imagine what it would feel like to lead a life like that, and to find an appropriate way to describe it "...lonely," he concluded, unable to find a better word.

"I imagine it is," replied Lucid gently. "Although she is incredibly wise, the Lady has only been with us, or indeed existed, for a few years. In normal terms she would still be considered a child and as a result she rarely leaves the house, for she finds much of the surrounding world and its complications far too disturbing to deal with."

As they spoke, they continued to make their way out of the house, Lucid leading them through a series of very similar-looking corridors that Adam struggled to remember from their arrival. He couldn't decide whether it was the disorientating effect of the house or his increasing tiredness which was making his brain ache as they walked.

"One more question, and I think quite a big one," asked Adam, as they drew close to the main door to the house, the soft carpeting giving way to heavy stone slabs. "What exactly is the Horror you kept talking about? It sounded important... and bad... really, really bad."

Lucid sighed, running a hand across his face, as if trying to manipulate his features back from their current glum state to his normal smile, but this time failing to do so.

"A Horror is what happens when a nightmare doesn't leave as it should do, instead it grows, losing its original form and becoming a whirling mass of misery and dark thoughts," Lucid said, continuing to scratch at his cheek absentmindedly as he spoke.

"The appearance of a Horror is itself a rarity, and if the rumours that Henry referred to have any basis in fact, the scale of this one is unprecedented. There hasn't been one of such a size during my time in the Five, although Grimble still remembers the last occasion we had to face one. They can be dealt with, but they are incredibly destructive and unpleasant."

Lucid finished scratching his cheek, appearing to try and clear his head and change the direction of their conversation at the same time.

"I appreciate your patience Adam, none of this was what I intended to show you when you came here. My aim was to try and introduce you to Reverie, give you any advice that I am capable of providing, and to fulfil your mother's wishes. The timing of your arrival and that of this gathering, which I am obliged to attend, was... unfortunate, but now it is concluded I will do what I can to make things up to you."

Adam nodded, his head starting to feel unnaturally heavy as he did so. As Lucid turned and began working on the complex series of bolts and deadlocks that secured the interior of the door back out to the gardens and then onwards to the City, Adam found it an increasing struggle to keep track of Lucid's movements. He could feel his eyelids drooping, suddenly fully aware of how very tired he felt and how long it had been since he had slept well.

Taking a slightly unsteady step towards the door, he tripped forward, stumbling over his own feet and heading face first towards the floor. As he fell his vision began to blur and fade, disappearing into a small dot of light in the centre of a swirl of darkness. He tensed, expecting a feeling of pain as he hit the stone slabs of the floor, but instead he felt his head sink gently into the softness and warmth of a pillow. Then his head cleared of the fog of sleep and his eyes snapped open, looking once again at the horrible wallpaper in Charlie's spare room.

CHAPTER 5

For several minutes Adam lay completely still, turning his recent memories over and over in his mind. He was lying in bed, he had just woken up, and he had obviously been dreaming. His brain told him all these things and yet he didn't quite believe the explanations the sensible part of his brain seemed determined to push into the rest of his head. Too many strange things had happened to him recently for him to accept logical explanations as willingly as he used to. He could still clearly recall the dream world, still visualise Grimble's scowl and Lucid's wide grinning face in vivid detail.

Pushing back his duvet he turned and sat on the side of the bed, putting the pendant he still had clutched protectively in his hand onto the bedside cabinet, then idly picked up a coin from the small pile of change he had emptied from his pocket the night before.

Turning it over and over in his hands he remembered Lucid's words, "Just think of the worlds as two sides of the same coin. In one world you are awake, whilst in the other you sleep." It had all seemed remarkably real and he felt a strange sense of loss now that he was awake and the dream had ended. But then again, his brain told him, arguing the case for the more sensible side of things once again, dreams always seemed real at the time and it was only when you woke up that the obvious impossibilities became clear.

"Adam," came a voice from outside the door, interrupting his train of thought, "we are just making breakfast, see you downstairs in ten minutes."

"Okay Mrs. Henson," Adam called back, placing the coin back

down on the table and rummaging around for some clothes. "I'll be down in a minute."

As he closed the bedroom door behind him and walked downstairs to the kitchen a couple of minutes later he decided that he would keep the adventures of last night to himself. The world of dreams, nightmares and strange lion creatures seemed so far removed from kitchen cabinets and laminate floor that, even if he still felt oddly connected to that world, he was convinced it would make absolutely no sense to anyone else. More likely they would think that the blow to the head he had suffered was having some sort of strange delayed effect on him.

"Morning Adam," said Charlie from his seat at the kitchen table, grinning through a mouthful of toast, "sorry for not waiting but I was really, really hungry." Then adding, as he crunched through the next slice, "How did you get on with your room, I thought it would be just your taste."

"Lovely thanks," replied Adam, ignoring the jibe "slept like a log." Not completely true admittedly, as logs almost certainly didn't have such odd dreams, but the answer seemed enough to satisfy Charlie and his parents, with Mr. and Mrs. Henson sharing a relieved smile that Adam just caught out the corner of his eye.

As he sat at the table and grabbed a couple of slices of toast for himself, topped up with a generous amount of jam, Mr. Henson sat down in the chair opposite him.

"Ignore Charlie," he said jovially, "if he carries on we'll make him swap rooms with you and see how long he copes with it. Personally, I could never stand that room, but Alice was insistent that was how she wanted it, or at least till she got to secondary school."

"She changed her mind then, quite radically," he added, grinning at the memory. "It's hard to be a Goth in a bright pink room, but sadly we never quite got around to redecorating. If you end up staying with us for a while we'll see if we can't do something to make it a bit less horrible, how about that?"

Adam nodded his thanks. "That would be very nice Mr. Henson, but honestly it's fine, it really doesn't bother me."

"Something else I was thinking," Mr. Henson continued, "you'll need to get some new things, like a new toothbrush, some spare shirts for school, that sort of thing. I thought that I could maybe run you and Charlie into the shops later and you could pick up a few bits?"

Although feeling a little embarrassed at accepting further generosity from the Hensons, Adam was also painfully aware of how little he had with him, the single suitcase he had unpacked being all that had survived the carnage at his home. Even the few things that he had brought with him, like his toothbrush and toothpaste, seemed a bit tainted and the thought of using them made him feel oddly sick.

"Thank-you," he said, "that would be great," before returning to his breakfast, the slight awkwardness of the moment quickly passing as they ate.

The closest and most convenient place for Charlie and Adam to do their shopping was a nearby shopping centre, where Mr. Henson dropped them, arranging to pick them up a couple of hours later. There was a large supermarket on the upper level and a parade of smaller chain stores on the ground floor. Even better there was also a small but excellent burger bar where he and Charlie would stop off whenever they had the money. With luck, and some careful purchases, Charlie was pretty hopeful they would have enough money left to fit in a quick visit before his dad collected them.

Just over an hour later, the first part of their shopping expedition was going exactly to plan. Adam had found most of the things he needed in the supermarket and Charlie had also managed to stay well within the budget his parents had set him. Congratulating each other on their economy the two made their way to the checkouts and were already focusing on their preferred burger, and if they could afford it, milkshake options.

As they passed the frozen food aisle Adam could feel the chill of the units, wishing for a moment he was wearing something warmer than his t-shirt, although Charlie seemed to be impervious to the same cold sensation.

Reaching the queue for the checkout Adam was still finding it unusually hard to shake the cold feeling, shivering despite his increasing distance from the chiller cabinets, but he put the thought to one side as he loaded his purchases onto the conveyor. The lady behind the counter returned Adam's smile with a bored stare as she scanned through his items and he stuffed them quickly into a carrier bag, aware of the spare time before Charlie's dad picked them up rapidly ticking away.

Quickly pocketing his handful of change, he turned to leave.

"Thanks Adam, have a nice day," the woman said as he began to walk away.

Sure that he hadn't given her his name, having only exchanged half a dozen words as he made his purchases, Adam half-turned back in confusion. He took a moment to look more closely at her face to see if it was perhaps more familiar than he had first thought, mentally going through the more obvious possibilities. Was she a friend of his mother's or maybe another parent from the school? Seemingly aware of his attention, the woman looked back across at him, and for a moment he found his gaze drawn to her eyes, where he could have sworn there was a momentary flicker of something strange, a glint of inky slick blackness so brief that he questioned whether he had really seen it.

"Adam," called Charlie, the sound of his voice breaking Adam's concentration, "come on, we haven't got long before dad arrives," and with that, the moment of strangeness passed.

"I thought..." Adam began, but Charlie was too far away to hear him properly, already on his way to the escalator and the alluring promise of fast food.

By the time he caught up with Charlie, Adam had convinced himself that his mind had been playing tricks on him. She must have been another parent from the school as he had first thought, he just hadn't recognised her.

Sitting with Charlie and eating an Empire Super Extra Deluxe Burger, (leaving out buying the milkshake so he could afford the biggest available burger having eventually been decided as a worthwhile trade-off), Adam felt the first moment of genuine pleasure he could recall since his return home nearly three weeks ago.

The combination of chatting with his best friend and the familiar surroundings, with memories of shared good times, allowed him to almost forget his troubles. He was able to push the weirdness of the last few days to the back of his mind and concentrate instead on enjoying time with his friend, even if only for a moment.

It was with a feeling of unavoidable regret that he stood to leave when Charlie signaled that it was time to go and get their lift back home, the weight of his problems settling immediately back onto his shoulders as he walked out the door.

❄ ❄ ❄

Much as he tried, that night Adam couldn't contain his nerves as he prepared for bed. As the rest of the day had gone on it had been harder and harder to make any reasonable sense of the strangeness of the previous night's dream, but that hadn't stopped his excitement building as the evening drew closer. Everything he had experienced the night before had been so vivid, so real and he had to admit so enthralling, that he desperately wanted it to have been something more than his sleeping mind playing strange tricks on him.

He had already made a mental deal with himself that tonight would be a test, he would go to bed, he would sleep, and he would see what happened. Despite this admirably scientific approach, a large part of him was still incredibly hopeful that sleep would bring a return to the dream world. It was therefore with great disappointment that Adam woke the next morning from a night of restless, but entirely dreamless, sleep.

The next couple of days passed in a very similar fashion, he had returned to school and aside from the occasional sympathetic or sometimes just outright curious look, life pretty much returned to a regular, although very different, pattern. In class he was back sitting next to Charlie in his normal seat, as Nora still hadn't made a reappearance. Increasingly surreal theories about her whereabouts or wellbeing working their way from person to person like a rumour transmitted flu virus.

"She had emigrated," or

"Her parents had left town in the middle of the night," or

"She was very ill with an incredibly rare tropical bug she had picked up on her travels that had turned her face bright blue and she was being kept in quarantine."

✻ ✻ ✻

Despite the increasing normality of his daily routine, each night Adam would mentally prepare himself for another entry into the strange world he had experienced, facing disappointment each morning when he awoke to the same view of the spare room following a night completely without dreams. It wasn't until the fourth night of empty sleep that a realisation hit him as he tossed and turned in bed, trying to get a pillow that was starting to feel more like a bag stuffed full of rocks than feathers into a more comfortable position.

Turning away from the wall, which he naturally tended to face as he fell asleep, his eyes settled on the bedside table and more specifically on the strange little pendant. His mind went back to the oddly warm feeling of the pendant in his hand as he had woken in the dream world. Knowing that it was probably ridiculous, but not particularly caring, he reached out and picked up the pendant, gripping it tightly. It took even longer than normal to get to sleep that night, but as sleep finally took him, rather than the emptiness of the previous nights, dreams once again filled his head.

CHAPTER 6

*In the centre of the room, bathed in a gentle yellow light suggesting
an imminent dawn, there is a small bed, wooden and simple. Although solidly built, the sides are slightly uneven and warped with
age. The sheets on the bed are crumpled, low peaks of cotton gathered
and scrunched, with a small head poking from the upper end.*

*Hair tousled, a young boy lies sleeping, but despite the crumpled
sheets and the messy hair, the sensation is of incredible age and per-
manence. The sheets crumpled an eternity ago, the hair tousled in a
completely different time. Now the only movement is a gentle breath
in, a pause, and then a matching breath out. Breathe in... the sun
rises, the tides flow, mountains slowly rise above the earth. Breathe
out... the sun sets, rivers slowly cut their way into the ground. Every
breath in and out matching perfectly in time, brow un-furrowed,
skin smooth and untroubled by worry.*

*Then ever so slightly, almost imperceptible, an eyelid flickers the
tiniest fraction. The smallest inkling of a shadow passing over the
sleeping face. As the eyelid moves the rest of the universe pauses, the
sun sits still in its orbit, the waves freeze in place. Then the next slow
breath in, the next steady breath out, and the world starts again.*

With a deep exhalation Adam opened his eyes, the strange
image of the sleeping boy still sharp in his mind. Once again he
could feel damp grass under his back, could see the surrounding
clearing, instantly recognised from his first arrival in Reverie.
This time the scene that met his eyes was more familiar to him,
the sight and scent of the giant yellow flowers less strange.

It was with a similar feeling of expectation that he turned
his head to one side and saw a figure watching him, lounging

comfortably in a folding wooden seat located on the edge of the clearing. He couldn't see the figure's features clearly, just a silhouette outlined in the morning sun. However, the lanky shape and ridiculously tall hat were enough of a giveaway on their own.

"Lucid?" Adam called out, half question, half greeting as he climbed to his feet.

"Glad to see you again Adam," Lucid replied, also standing and then pointing to his seat, which Adam could now see was plumped out with several large and brightly coloured cushions.

"I am also happy to say I have learnt from my past mistakes and made sure to bring a far more comfortable seat to rest upon whilst awaiting your return."

Several strides from his long legs and Lucid was by Adam's side. Now he was stood more closely, while the smile on Lucid's face was familiar to Adam from their last meeting, the dark circles under his eyes were not.

"But don't mistake my more comfortable seating arrangements as anything other than that, while my body has been more rested my mind has not found any such peace since you left our world so suddenly."

Lucid reached out a hand for a moment as if to place it upon Adam's shoulder, before appearing to change his mind and letting it drop back to his side instead.

"I must admit that I was starting to worry. You left before I had the chance to tell you everything I meant to..."

Lucid paused, the smile dropping out of his eyes, even if not fully leaving his mouth, as he restarted his sentence. "...before I had the chance to tell you everything that I should have. I fear that I failed in my duties during our first meeting, I intend to make up for that."

This time the walk to Nocturne seemed to pass far more quickly, and in the time it took for them to travel from the clearing to the City gates Lucid managed to fill Adam in on all that had passed since they had last met. To his surprise this time

Adam felt no doubt or sense of disbelief, rather he found himself completely at ease as they walked together, oddly comfortable in his acceptance of such bizarre circumstances.

There was still no news from Maya, the scout who had been missing at the last meeting, which clearly continued to trouble Lucid, although he quickly moved on to a different topic and Adam decided not to press him. He did, however, take the chance to describe to Lucid the unusual vision he had experienced before he had re-awoken in Reverie. He described the small room, the bed, and the sleeping child.

"It was so strange," Adam said, "he was only a boy, but he seemed really old at the same time... does that make any sense?"

"It does," replied Lucid quietly. "You are very fortunate. I believe you may have seen, just for a moment, the Dreamer himself."

"The Dreamer," repeated Adam, the way Lucid had said the name seemed unusually respectful.

"This is not a particularly religious world," Lucid continued, "and there is not much in the way of organised belief here, but most agree that the world in which we now walk is the dream of one universal and powerful being, so we refer to him as the Dreamer. Occasionally, if someone has a particularly strong connection to this world, they may have a glancing vision of the Dreamer and this is always the same. A small boy, sleeping peacefully exactly as you describe."

Putting his hand on to Adam's shoulder Lucid gently turned him to one side and pointed towards the horizon. Far in the distance, through the slight haze, Adam could vaguely make out an impossibly tall slim structure jutting out from the ground and rising high into the sky. From this distance it appeared to reach beyond the clouds, disappearing from sight. Until a few days ago Adam would have considered it completely impossible that such a thing could exist. He may not have paid as much attention as he should have during science lessons, but even he had picked up enough to know that there was no way that the thing he was looking at should be able to exist, let alone stay standing.

"That…" Lucid explained, his voice as calm and gentle as the expression that now crossed his face, "…is the Stairway of Dreams. If there is a centre to all belief, then that is it. Most consider that the Stairway must lead directly to the Dreamer himself, although no one has ever climbed to the top of the stairs, which seem to stretch infinitely into the sky."

"But enough of these things," he continued, as his voice returned to its normal and more jaunty tone. "We have more immediate issues to discuss. How have things been in your world Adam? Your mother was afraid for you, and as a result, so were we all. When you didn't return the night following your first visit I began to fear the worst, yet here you are alive and well."

"Everything is just normal…" Adam replied "…or at least as normal as it can be at the moment."

He could feel a lump forming in his throat as he continued, letting his guard down for a moment.

"I miss my mum. I worry about her all the time… but I haven't felt like I'm in any danger since she went missing. I just do normal stuff, I go to school, I see my friends, go to the shops."

He concentrated, thinking back for a moment, trying his best to focus on something other than his mother.

"Actually there was one thing, one time when I thought I saw something unusual."

Lucid looked across at him questioningly, prompting Adam to continue despite his reservations.

"There was a lady at the shop I went to who knew my name… although I'm pretty sure I didn't know her… and I thought for a moment I saw something strange in her eyes."

At this Lucid visibly stiffened, turning to give Adam his full attention. "Tell me, describe what you saw."

"It was… weird," Adam continued, "but just for a second I thought I saw something odd in her eyes, it was kind of inky looking?" He paused, realising how little he could actually tell Lucid and how ridiculous it all sounded now he said it out loud.

"I am sure it was just my eyes playing tricks on me. I was

stood quite a long way from her and couldn't even see her eyes that well."

But it was clear from Lucid's reaction that he thought differently. His eyes had narrowed at Adam's words and he muttered something under his breath.

"What is it?" asked Adam, now more concerned.

"An Incubo…" There was a hint of venom in Lucid's voice.

"What you describe could be an Incubo. They are a waking nightmare, a bad dream that gets inside of someone and lives within them even when they are awake. Fortunately, it's never for long, and often the unlucky victim doesn't even realise, just remembers a period when they had particularly bad dreams or felt unusually unhappy."

Adam shuddered at the thought as Lucid continued.

"As you saw before, most Nightmares are mindless beings but an Incubo is intelligent, and not just that, they can communicate and are capable of working with others. A particularly strong one can even completely take over its host for a short while. They are absolutely the worst kind of Nightmare, although thankfully they are also very rare."

"I might have been mistaken," said Adam, trying to hold on to his previous, although now increasingly fragile, belief that there had been nothing to be worried about. "I only saw something for a moment."

"You might," Lucid replied. "An Incubo is incredibly hard to spot, especially if you don't know what you are looking for. They hide themselves well, but the inner darkness and misery they cause can sometimes be seen in the eyes of their victim."

Lucid beckoned for Adam to follow him once again. "However this coincidence is too great to risk ignoring. Come with me back to the house, there is something I will need to show you."

The rest of the walk to the Mansion passed in a rather spiky silence, Lucid unusually distracted, walking with a sense of even greater urgency than Adam remembered from their previous meetings. Within a few minutes they were standing in the Hallway, having been let in this time by a far less surly gatekeeper than during their last visit. A pleasant old lady called Mrs. Snugs who seemed to be responsible for the general upkeep and running of the sprawling home had ushered them in, although Lucid had been so preoccupied that they hardly paused to say hello.

As they approached the Dining Room, Lucid drew to a halt in the portrait corridor by one of the more recent paintings and pointed to one of the individuals within it, Adam recognising the painting immediately from his first visit. It was the first of the three that had included Grimble and showed him as a younger and far more cheerful version of himself. However, it wasn't Grimble that Lucid drew his attention to. Instead, he pointed to a tall, handsome man who was stood to Grimble's immediate left, white-blonde and smiling broadly, his hand resting on Grimble's shoulder companionably.

"That is, or more correctly was, Isenbard," said Lucid. Adam unconsciously dropped his eyes to the plaque below the portrait and saw the name had been neatly crossed through with a thick, black line.

"He was a legend amongst us, a great hero of the Five... and perhaps, more importantly, a close friend to Grimble. Many years ago, well before my time, there was another appearance of a Horror and the Five gathered to deal with it. While they are always serious, Horrors have previously been dealt with without great incident by our predecessors, however, this time things went very, very wrong. Although I don't know all the details, and Grimble will rarely speak of it, I do know that Isenbard turned on his friends just as they tried to face the Horror, putting them all in terrible danger."

Lucid sighed heavily, "Grimble swears that the moment before the betrayal he saw the darkness you spoke of in his friend's eyes and believes to this day that an Incubo had taken him over. He has never quite recovered from the experience and now he hates the Nightmares, and Incubo in particular, more than you can imagine."

"What happened to him?" asked Adam, his eyes still drawn to the man's face, the friendly smile and the lively, intelligent-looking eyes captured forever by the artist's brushstrokes.

"He disappeared into the Horror just before it was destroyed," replied Lucid shivering slightly, "a terrible fate for anyone to suffer."

Pausing for a final moment to look once more at the portrait before leaving the corridor, Lucid led Adam through the Dining Room and past the large table where the previous meeting had taken place, opening a smaller door in the far wall.

Following Lucid through the doorway, Adam immediately felt the morning sun on his face. Tall painted wooden beams framed large glazed panels which welcomed in the sunlight, filling the room with golden warmth. The conservatory they had walked into was full of random pieces of incidental furniture with groupings of mismatched but comfy looking chairs around small tables, and a series of large heavily cushioned sofas along the back wall, positioned to make the most of the natural light.

Lucid lowered himself into one of the more comfortable looking chairs closest to the door with a contented sigh and motioned for Adam to do the same. Reaching across to the wall he pulled on a chain hanging from the ceiling and Adam thought he could hear the very faint ringing of a bell somewhere in the house.

"This is absolutely my favourite room," said Lucid with a degree of satisfaction. "Whatever troubles or worries I have, and the Dreamer knows that we have our share at the moment, this room always helps settle my mind and lets me think."

Adam had taken the seat opposite Lucid and was surprised at how comfortable the small chair was, feeling like it had been designed to fit him perfectly. From where he had chosen to sit you could see through the large windows into the gardens of the house, which sprawled far into the distance, making it easy to forget you were in the middle of a large, busy City. As he settled back into the seat enjoying the warmth of the sun on his face and the contrast from the recent dark topics of conversation, Adam was slightly, although extremely pleasantly, surprised by the appearance of Mrs. Snugs bustling into the room carrying a tray loaded with a variety of breakfasts and drinks.

"Thank you Mrs. Snugs, as always you look after me far too well," said Lucid with a wide and contented grin, his eyes already taking in the mound of food she placed on the table between them.

"You're welcome Mr. Lucid, I am sure you need feeding up after all those days waiting out in the fields, you poor thing," replied Mrs. Snugs, blushing slightly and then giving Adam a quick smile before bustling back out of the room again. Although Adam had only seen her a couple of times it was already clear to him that 'bustle' was the only speed that Mrs. Snugs operated at.

"She exaggerates my hardships," said Lucid happily, as he picked a warm bread roll from the tray and started to spread it with a thick layer of butter. "Every day that I was waiting for you in the field she packed me a picnic with more delicious food than you could hope for. If it hadn't been for my worry it would have been a very pleasant way for me to pass my time."

Adam leant forward to help himself to some of the food, picking a warm pastry filled with sweet spiced fruit.

"You must try the hot chocolate," said Lucid, pausing his enthusiastic munching for a moment to point to the large jug in the middle of the tray, "Mrs. Snugs makes it herself and it is truly exceptional."

The chocolate was indeed every bit as good as Lucid had promised. Thick, creamy and delicious, it left a strange but pleasant lingering warmth at the back of Adam's throat long after he had finished it.

Despite the circumstances of his visit to the house, Adam couldn't help but feel a sense of temporary contentment as he placed his mug on the table and sat back in his chair. Lucid had also finished his breakfast and with obvious regret put down his empty plate.

"Pleasant an interlude as that was," he sighed, "we must now return to the more serious business at hand. It is clear that you will need to return to your world whenever you sleep here and so I cannot keep you safe all of the time. What I can do is inform you of the dangers you may face and prepare you as well as I can for the times we are apart, particularly now I fear that an Incubo may have somehow crossed into your world."

He rummaged for a moment in the various pockets inside his coat and handed Adam a small bag. "Even after all these years we haven't found much which is effective, but this bag contains a mix of herbs which we have discovered, when burned, releases a fragrance that will temporarily repel Nightmares."

Adam took the bag and sniffed it gingerly, getting a slight whiff of aniseed and other less familiar smells.

"Grimble claims that the bag has been treated in such a way that it can travel safely back with you into the waking world, although I suppose only time will tell if that is correct. Unfortunately, there is little more I can give you physically that will aid your protection, so the most important thing is to help you learn as much as you can," Lucid continued.

"As I told you when you first arrived here, if you have inherited your mother's talents then you are a Daydreamer, and that is by far your most important asset. Far more useful than any bag of herbs, or for that matter any other thing I could give you."

"I know you said about it before, and that it was important but I don't even know what being a Daydreamer really means... or at least what it means here," Adam admitted, intrigued but not really understanding what Lucid was trying to tell him.

Brushing stray crumbs from his coat and trousers Lucid rose to his feet. "I think that it might be easier for me to show you than try to explain."

He pointed to the wide double doors leading from the conservatory into the gardens of the house.

"Perhaps it would be best if we continued this particular discussion outside."

Lucid directed Adam to a wide area of well-mown grass, between two large borders of extremely unusual plants. To one side there was a mass of tangled creepers, climbing the high brick boundary walls. Looking closely the creepers seemed to be slowly moving, a constant dark green mass winding around each other in a continuous dance. While it initially hurt his eyes watching the plant, Adam found he could roughly keep track of the steady churn of its movement by following the progress of the occasional buds or flower heads that dotted the main body of the creepers.

To the other side, between the grassed lawn area and the house, was a wider border filled with a variety of bushy plants. These alternated between large, soft-looking leaves and taller, slim stems topped by dots of vibrantly coloured flower heads. Despite the lack of breeze, these swayed gently from side to side, and if Adam strained his hearing, he was almost certain he could hear a soft tinkling sound that seemed to be keeping time with the swaying movement.

Lucid interrupted Adam's distracted stare with a polite tap on the shoulder. "I wouldn't look at those for too long," he said, "they are a very pretty but also rather hypnotic species, if you're not careful you could stand there all day and night before you realise it."

Adam shook his head, clearing the cobwebs that seemed to have suddenly formed in his brain, and turned back to face Lucid.

"Now I have your attention again, let me explain to you further what being a Daydreamer means in this world," continued Lucid. "I want you to think about what happens when you dream, what you become, and most of all what you can achieve."

Adam nodded and tried to think back to some of his recent dreams.

"In your dreams you can do impossible things," Lucid explained. "Time is different, you can fall incredible distances, walk up walls, even fly!"

It was true, Adam had to admit, while some of his dreams were very normal and boring, similar to his everyday life, others were full of adventures where he was able to do things that he knew were impossible in real life.

"Okay," Adam said slowly, "but that's just in my dreams."

"Exactly," replied Lucid, emphasising his statement with an enthusiastic click of his long fingers. "And you are now conscious and aware within Reverie, where someone like you or your mother can, with enough effort, do all of those impossible things."

"That ridiculous," said Adam, although at the back of his mind a persistent and increasingly loud voice was already nagging at him and telling him that:

1. He had done all those things, and more, within his dreams;

2. He was in a dream world called Reverie speaking with impossible people so, as far as common sense was concerned, all bets were off;

3. It would be incredibly, fantastically cool.

"It's easy enough to prove," said Lucid, appearing to be as excited to prove his point as Adam was to see if Lucid was correct. "And as time is short, I suggest that we go straight to something significant. So if you will indulge me, please could you close your eyes and concentrate on the feeling you had in a recent dream, one in which you did something fantastical."

Despite feeling highly self-conscious, Adam did as he was asked, closed his eyes and tried to recall a dream in which he had achieved impossible things. He slowly let his mind settle, blocking out the gentle sounds of the garden lingering in the background. As he relaxed and let his thoughts start to drift, one dream jumped to the front of his mind, one of his absolute favourites that still made him smile to think of it.

After a particularly exciting story his Mother had told him about superheroes and villains, he had spent a joyful night dreaming of flying high above a crime-riddled City, thwarting villains and generally having the time of his life. Still, while the recollection was one which brought back happy memories and for a moment even made him forget the oddness of his current circumstances, it remained nothing more than a pleasant memory.

Opening his eyes again to explain this to Lucid and to ask if this was the kind of dream he was looking for, Adam was utterly disoriented by the view that now faced him. Rather than the edges of the lawn or the planted borders of the garden, he found himself looking directly at the second storey of the ancient house. Immediately panicking, his eyes darted around trying to make sense of this new and unexpected perspective. Looking straight down proved to be a particular mistake, finding his feet standing on nothing, and perhaps even worse, seeing Lucid's upturned face gawping in delighted amazement almost directly below him.

His feeling of contended memory completely gone, he could feel himself wobbling and started to flap his arms in a vain attempt to stabilise himself, although this had little effect other than making him feel particularly foolish as well as terrified.

Looking ahead again he realised he could see directly into the upstairs room he was now hovering outside. Facing him from within the room was the glowing figure of the Lady, her hands resting on the sill of the open window. Her sharp blue eyes locked with his for a moment and almost immediately he felt the last of any limited control he had over his movements drain away as he began to tumble towards the ground.

A few seconds later and his viewpoint had changed once again, and he now found himself looking up through a canopy of dark green leaves into Lucid's concerned face. However, as soon as Adam had confirmed that he was okay, other than a few minor scratches and bruises achieved on the way down, the look of concern was replaced by jubilation.

"Ha-ha... I knew it," Lucid crowed. "I knew you were a Daydreamer. I absolutely, positively knew it. I could feel it as soon as I met you and now..." he wound down to a halt without finishing the sentence, apparently overwhelmed by the sheer exuberance of his mood.

"That was... impossible," Adam managed to stammer, still shaken by the suddenness of everything that he had just gone through.

"Impossible for most..." replied Lucid ecstatically, bouncing lightly from foot to foot with barely contained excitement "... but not for you." He paused for a moment to help Adam get gingerly to his feet. "Although," he added, "you might need a little more practice before we try something like that again."

"Good idea," Adam agreed, deciding that sitting back down in the conservatory for a while would be quite the nicest thing to do. At least till his legs stopped wobbling like jelly, his breathing settled down and his stomach returned to its normal place.

While Adam sat and collected himself, Lucid continued to pace restlessly around the room as he spoke. "I appreciate that this must seem, at the very least, unusual to you. It must be hard to understand and to accept, but this is exactly the same process your mother went through all those years ago."

Lucid's mouth twisted in amusement as he continued. "Well perhaps not exactly the same, it was several weeks before she tried something as foolhardy as flying... and it went rather better than your first attempt."

"Regardless," he continued "as I said before, knowledge of what you are capable of is also absolutely the best defence I can give you, far better than any physical protection. So, as soon as you feel ready, I suggest we continue."

The rest of the day passed with far less incident, Adam restricting himself to more conservative applications of his new-found abilities. By the time lunch arrived, wheeled in on a large but rickety hostess trolley by Mrs. Snugs, Adam was feeling pretty pleased with himself, having managed to knock Lucid's hat from his head several times, albeit rather weakly, using nothing but the forceful application of his imagination.

Lucid had been somewhat less impressed by this and now sat rather morosely, trying to straighten out a small but unsightly crease in the hat's brim. However, his mood was greatly improved at the sight of the sheer quantity of hearty food that Mrs. Snugs had somehow managed to squeeze onto the trolley.

Even better than that, by the end of the day, as evening started to draw in, Adam had overcome his initial nerves about trying to fly again. After several unsuccessful attempts, reflected in a series of deep scuffs in the lawn, two broken plant pots and Mrs. Snugs having to make a most unladylike dive into the nearest hedge, he had managed to maintain an unsteady hover for a few seconds, careful to stay no more than a metre from the ground.

With this success under their belt, Lucid decided to call it a day, and as the last of the sunlight faded from the garden, he followed Adam back into the conservatory.

"Night is coming, and you've had a long and tiring day," Lucid said, stifling a yawn himself. "Soon enough you will have to sleep and you will awake back in your world."

He directed Adam to take a seat on one of the large sofas as he continued to speak. "You have achieved a great deal today but it is only a beginning, so please be careful. Even your mother, who was an incredibly accomplished Daydreamer, was afraid of something that had come into your world, so do not be complacent even for a moment. There are much greater threats in existence than you are capable of dealing with, and while you are away from Reverie, I cannot protect or aid you."

Although kindly meant, Lucid's words quickly deflated the rush of excitement and accomplishment that Adam had been feeling. As he sat back on the soft cushions of the sofa the realisation that he would soon be awake again in the real world, where he would go back to a far more regular life, was also something that was surprisingly hard to deal with.

Lucid seemed to pick up on some of Adam's worry. "I appreciate that this world is all new to you and that many things are strange, but a great deal of knowledge about the dreaming world has bled over into yours though time, contained within myths or old stories."

He paused and patted Adam on the shoulder reassuringly.

"It would be a good use of your time to try and find some of these stories in your world, then perhaps next time you come here I think it would benefit you to also visit our library, there is someone there you should meet."

Adam nodded and found himself yawning as he did so, the soft cushions proving to be increasingly hard to resist. "I'll leave you to sleep," said Lucid and walked quietly from the conservatory. "Take good care Adam."

Despite the excitement of the day, the tiredness that Adam felt in combination with the deep comfort of the sofa as he lay back and rested his head meant that soon enough his eyes dropped closed.

CHAPTER 7

When Adam opened his eyes again to the familiar sight of the guest room, this time he felt far less doubt about the experiences of the previous night. Instead, he lay still for a few minutes re-running everything that had happened in his mind before deciding to get up. As he rolled to one side to get out of bed, he felt a sharp prickle in his leg and looking down saw a small cotton bag, tied tightly closed at the top.

Picking it up and lifting it to his nose, he gingerly sniffed it. As he suspected he got the whiff of aniseed along with less familiar smells, recognising it as the bag that Lucid had given him for protection against the Nightmares. Carefully he placed the bag on the bedside table alongside his pendant and sat for a long moment staring at them both, his chin resting in his hands. Despite his increasing belief in the dream world, the sight of the small bag was still the first actual proof that it was real. Adam breathed in deeply, letting it sink in... it was all real, unbelievable and very, very odd, but somehow still real.

While he could have sat there for much longer, just savouring this new realisation, Adam knew that outside his door the rest of the world was waiting and there were things he needed to do. So after a minute he lifted the pendant and placed it around his neck, feeling a faint glow of warmth for a moment as it touched his skin, and pocketed the small bag.

Charlie immediately noticed Adam's distraction as they ate breakfast. "You sleep all right?" he said. "You look a bit tired."

"Hmmm? – oh yeah, fine thanks," Adam responded a little shortly, not really paying attention. His mind was still replaying the previous night's events, and in particular, recalling

Lucid's last piece of advice to him.

"Do you think we could go to the library today?" Adam asked.

"Sure, I suppose," Charlie replied, "what did you want to go for?"

Adam thought that the genuine reason, to look into myths that might relate to the dream world, to Nightmares and Horrors, might be a bit hard to explain. So instead he said, "I thought I could do a bit more research for my family tree project, we're back at school tomorrow and I've got quite a bit left to do."

"We can pop over after breakfast if you want then," said Charlie reaching across to do a quick search on his phone. "Looks like it opens at ten o'clock on a Sunday."

Adam spent the next hour trying to make normal conversation, only partly paying attention while his mind was already rushing ahead to the end of the day and his next chance to revisit Reverie. Despite his distraction the time passed quickly enough and by ten o'clock he and Charlie were waiting patiently outside the local library.

"Miss. Grudge wouldn't believe it if she could see you now," said Charlie, looking across at Adam with an expression which had hardly changed from bemused since Adam had first suggested the visit to the library.

"That's not fair," replied Adam indignantly, "I go to the library all the time."

"True, I suppose," Charlie admitted, "but have you ever gone to do school-work before, rather than pick up new stories or comics?"

Adam started to respond, realised he couldn't think of a good answer and was fortunately saved from further embarrassment by the sight of the librarian opening the front doors.

"Bang on ten o'clock," said Charlie approvingly. "That's what I like to see, a really punctual librarian."

Adam sighed theatrically at this. One of Charlie's very few oddities was his belief that people should always act exactly like the television stereotype of their job. Nurses should be kind and cheerful, salesmen should be smooth and slightly oily, and presumably librarians should be punctual, a little bit dowdy, wear glasses on a string around their neck and say "shhhh!" all the time.

Walking straight through the fiction section they made their way to the stairs that led up to the reference library. So soon after opening time on a Sunday the library was still deserted, giving them the whole floor pretty much to themselves. The only other person up with them was the trainee librarian behind the desk at the back of the room, and despite the library having only been open two minutes she was already looking bored.

The trainee was a girl in her late teens, who much to Charlie's annoyance was very pretty, had shaggy purple hair and at least one visible tattoo, had occasionally been late for work and had never once said "shhhh" to either of them.

"Where do we start then?" asked Charlie, keen to get whatever boring research was necessary out the way as quickly as possible, so they could get on with the more fun part of the day.

Adam stopped and gave it a quick thought. He didn't really want Charlie looking over his shoulder while he researched dreams and nightmares.

"Could you have a look through the books on local history?" asked Adam. "All the family members my mum found for me lived miles away and I was hoping I could find a reference to my family a bit closer to home."

He paused. "I know it's a long shot, but just in case there is anything it would be really helpful."

While he didn't think for a minute there really would be anything there, the local history section was in a far corner of the room and Adam thought it would give him some space to do his actual research more privately.

"Okay," said Charlie, a little doubtfully, "I don't think there will be anything, but I will have a look if you want."

Feeling pretty bad about misleading his friend, Adam awkwardly smiled his thanks and made his way to the other end of the room. Although it took a few minutes he managed to find two books which looked promising, one covering ancient folk tales and another on superstitions and folk remedies.

Taking both books to a nearby study desk along with a further book on genealogy, opened to a random page to give him a decent cover story if Charlie came back over, Adam began to quickly read his way through them.

Within a few pages he could already see the truth of Lucid's words. Many of the things that he had seen in Reverie were there, in one form or another, hidden away just below the surface in old folk tales. Looking at pictures of Goblins or Kobolds you could almost see the short, stocky figure and hard features of Grimble, although only if you were to remove the gruff humanity and intelligence that Adam remembered. It was like the authors of the fables had recorded half-remembered details from dreams of their own. But the creatures in the book were unflattering reflections of the beings Adam had met in Reverie, distorted unpleasantly as if viewed in a fairground mirror.

The other book on superstitions also turned out to be interesting, with a section on old folk remedies referring to Anise as a cure for nightmares, explaining the scent of Aniseed Adam had been getting from the small bag Lucid had given him. However, despite this, nothing that Adam had found so far added anything new to his knowledge, it just confirmed things that he had already been told. Then, as he turned to a new chapter on folk remedies and beliefs from around the world, his eye was caught by the image of a Native American dreamcatcher.

The dreamcatcher in the picture was fairly small, a little over 3 inches in size, hanging over the crib of a small baby. The accompanying text explaining that, according to Native American legends, the first dreamcatchers were made by 'Asibikaashi' or the Spider Woman, to keep young children safe from nightmares and give them good dreams. Traditionally made from willow hoops, they had a spider web of red-dyed thread tied across them, replicating the protective webs originally weaved by the Spider Woman.

Adam quickly wrote down as much as he could, wondering if it was another example of something that had come over from Reverie and deciding to ask Lucid when he saw him again. As he finished writing he saw Charlie walking back over, so he quickly snapped the book closed and turned his notebook to a blank page.

"Hi Charlie," he said, doing his best to not look too guilty, but Charlie seemed too distracted to notice.

"Um, I think I have found something," Charlie told him with a worried look, "but I don't think it was what you were expecting."

"What is it?" asked Adam, pushing the book on superstitions further behind him as he did so.

"I found this," said Charlie, still looking worried. "It was totally by chance. I was looking through the local history section like you asked and there were some old newspapers on one of the racks at the side." He held out a paper for Adam to take. "It was on the front page and I thought I recognised the picture."

Adam looked down and for a moment couldn't spot what Charlie was talking about, seeing no reference to his family. Then he realised what Charlie meant, the bottom right of the paper had a black and white picture of a serious-faced woman stood in front of a cottage. Pulling his family tree project from his rucksack Adam took out the photo of Cousin Penelope that his mother had given him and placed it alongside the newspaper, the two pictures matching identically. His eye was drawn to the caption under the photograph, 'Local author Susan Meredith talks about her latest novel'. He looked again at the family tree to make sure he wasn't mistaken, sure enough it was the same image but with the name Cousin Penelope underneath.

"I don't understand," said Adam, "it's definitely the same picture, but the name, everything else is different."

Charlie was still looking worried as he replied. "Sorry Adam, I didn't know whether to show you... but I thought I recognised the picture from your project and that it might be a lead for researching your family tree... then I read the article."

Looking again between the two pictures Adam couldn't see any possible explanation other than the most troubling one.

"My mum lied to me," said Adam in disbelief, "this isn't a member of my family at all." He looked back at the family tree he had so carefully put together, eyes settling for a moment on each of the other pictures. "Are any of these real?" he added, half to himself. His previous excitement at having found some new information related to the dream world was completely gone, replaced instead by confusion and a strangely empty feeling in his stomach.

"I don't think I want to do any more research," Adam said despondently, "do you mind if we just go home?"

"Of course not," Charlie replied, still looking awkward. "Look, I'm really sorry, maybe I shouldn't have..."

"No, its fine," Adam cut in. "I'd rather know, I just wish I understood why she lied to me about my family. Come on, let's go."

As they approached the desk close to the main entrance the Head Librarian looked up. "Hello Adam, how are you, have you had any news on your mother yet?" he asked, a concerned look on his face.

"No... nothing, thanks for asking," Adam responded automatically and then wondered for a moment how the Librarian knew about his mum's disappearance.

"Are you sure you don't know where she might be?" the Librarian continued as they drew closer. "I would have thought that if anyone would know it would be you."

"No, I told you I don't know," replied Adam again, this time more forcefully as he made his way towards the exit, passing the Librarian on his way out.

As he walked past, Adam could feel a chill in the air and an icy cold sensation at the back of his neck. An unpleasant feeling that he was starting to recognise.

"I would really like to find her Adam..." the Librarian said, straightening up slowly behind the desk as he spoke, "...and I think you might not be telling me everything."

Adam span around at this and looked at the Librarian directly, his eyes drawn immediately to the man's face. For a moment he thought he saw a flash of inky blackness cross the pupils of his eyes, as he had with the lady at the checkout in the supermarket, but this time he didn't doubt what he had seen.

"Come on Charlie," he said, backing away towards the exit, "we need to leave."

"What's going on Adam?" he heard Charlie say behind him, his voice a little higher pitched than normal, sounding confused and edged with worry.

"Nothing to worry about," Adam reassured him, although not very convincingly, his voice equally shaky, "I just think we should leave."

By this point the Librarian had vaulted over the front desk, with far more athleticism than a middle-aged man in a cardigan should ever have been capable of, and was now striding towards them both.

"We should leave right now," Adam said, picking up the nearest book from the returns trolley and throwing it as hard as he could in the librarian's direction, then turning and running out of the main entrance without stopping to see if the book had hit its target or not. Within moments he was out of the library and on his way down the stone steps outside, with Charlie now running alongside him.

"Seriously," gasped Charlie from beside him, "what's going on? You just threw a book at the Librarian!" He paused mid-sentence for a moment as they ran around the corner of the road into the next street. "Who, I admit, was acting a bit odd," he continued in between deep breaths.

Adam risked a look back over his shoulder, the street behind them appeared to be empty of vengeful librarians, so he slowed to a walk.

"Some very strange things have been happening to me lately," he admitted, turning to face his friend, "ever since my mum went missing."

Charlie nodded, "I know that what happened at your house

was terrible, it would mess with anybody's head."

Adam shook his head, "No, it's not that... or I mean it's not all that, there are other things since then... but you wouldn't believe me if I told you."

"Try me," Charlie replied, then his eyes widened as he spotted something behind Adam. "But maybe later," he added, pointing to the approaching figure of the Librarian. "You must have really annoyed him, he's still chasing us."

"I will try and explain, honestly," said Adam, "but for now I think we should run again," and they set off down the street, weaving between other pedestrians and narrowly avoiding a young mum with a double buggy.

Halfway down the street, they reached an alley which provided a cut through to the road next to Charlie's house. Without pausing they both turned and ran through it, Adam's eyes fixed on the end of the alley just ahead. They were perhaps ten metres away from reaching it when the feeling hit him.

Everything around him started to slow down, the rush of the air past his ears as he ran quietening, the sound of the busy road ahead fading into the background. As this happened, he also found it increasingly difficult to move, suddenly feeling like he was running through thick mud up to his knees.

"There's no running from me boy," came a cold, calm voice from behind him and turning his head slowly to look back over his shoulder, Adam could see the silhouetted figure of the Librarian. He was walking unhurriedly down the alleyway towards the spot where Adam and Charlie were now frozen in place. The feeling of helplessness was complete and awful, reminding Adam of the very worst of his bad dreams.

Not those with monsters or other terrible things, far worse than these were the nightmares where he was running from some unseen creature, some unknown threat. As he ran, in those most terrifying of dreams, he would feel his energy slowly draining away, his momentum failing. Sooner or later he would stop moving and find himself stuck on the spot, unable to do anything other than wait for whatever it was that was chasing him to inevitably catch up. But in his dreams, just as his pursuer was about to reach him, as the tension was impossible to stand a moment longer, he would always wake up. This time Adam didn't think that was likely to happen, this time the monster was going to catch him, and he felt powerless to stop it.

Although it took intense effort, he was able to turn away from the slowly advancing Librarian, looking across at Charlie again. His friend's expression was frozen in a look of confusion, only his eyes desperately darting back and forth revealed the true extent of his panic. More than anything else at that moment Adam wanted to apologise to his friend for putting him in danger but was unable to say anything, the effort of forming words too much for him to manage.

The chill he had felt earlier had returned and was now so intense it was becoming physically painful. His breath was becoming shorter and it was starting to feel like too much effort to even keep his eyes open.

"Adam, Adam, Adam, whatever should I do with you," the cold voice returned, now very close to Adam's ear, its tone light and mocking. "I ask you a perfectly reasonable question, show concern about your dear mother and you repay me by running."

The Librarian circled Adam for a moment as he continued to speak. "I told you, there is no running away from me. If you won't willingly give me the answers I am looking for, then I am afraid that I will have to take them from you."

Slowly and deliberately the Librarian rolled back the sleeves of his shirt and flexed his fingers. Darkness, similar to that which Adam had briefly seen in the Librarian's eyes, but more solid, more substantial, gathered at the end of his fingers. Then the Librarian raised his arms and the darkness began to stretch out from the fingertips towards Adam in long spindly tendrils.

Adam wasn't sure what was going to happen to him when the coiling darkness reached him, but he was convinced that it would not be good. Still, he was determined to fight whatever it was with any remaining strength he had left, and as the first dark strand brushed his cheek he tensed himself.

Then just as he gritted his teeth, preparing for the worst, he felt a burning heat from his chest and looking down saw a bright glow through his t-shirt centred on the spot where the pendant hung. There was a pulse of light, so bright that the afterglow flickered across his vision after he instinctively squeezed his eyes closed and a deep, loud voice echoed in Adam's mind. "Run!"

Almost immediately Adam found that the previous paralysis that had affected him had gone and he could see the Librarian staggering back, apparently blinded and disorientated by the light. Without pausing to think he grabbed Charlie's arm and dragged him to the end of the alleyway and out into the street. From just behind him he heard an animalistic shout of fury, and although he thought he was already running about as fast as he could, he somehow managed to find a bit more speed, still pulling Charlie along behind him. Risking a quick look back over his shoulder he could see the Librarian, now on the street behind them and rapidly gaining ground. Adam looked around desperately, realising that there was no way that they could reach Charlie's house before the Librarian caught up with them, and even worse than that, that the house was unlikely to offer any sort of safety even if they could get there.

Looking across at the small row of shops halfway down the street he had the start of an idea. Turning suddenly to the left, nearly pulling Charlie's arm out of its socket with the unexpected change of direction, he pushed his way through the door of a small café. He weaved past the café's elderly waitress, spinning her on the spot and making her spill the cup of tea she had been carefully carrying, creating a light brown sugary fountain that just missed his head. Without pausing, although taking the time to shout a quick "sorry!" as he passed, Adam dashed through the back door leading to the kitchen, just as the Librarian burst through the entrance, now only a few metres behind them.

The back of the café was currently empty but to Adam's relief and delight there was a pan boiling gently on the gas hob.

Without looking back Adam grabbed the bag of herbs from his pocket and threw it towards the open flame of the hob, before yanking open the back door to the kitchen. It wasn't until he had dragged Charlie out of the door after him that he finally risked another backward glance, with the view stopping him in his tracks.

The Librarian was stood in the middle of the kitchen, completely still other than a violent trembling that was running up and down his body. The tendrils of darkness that had previously emerged from his fingers were now flailing randomly from his hands, and to Adam's surprise and disgust also started to emerge from his eyes, mouth, and nose. The room was rapidly filling with acrid smoke from the burning herbs, which was gathering thickly around the Librarian, seeming to be drawn to the strands of darkness. A few moments later the dark tendrils started to dissipate, losing their previous substance and turning to ragged black wisps, before disappearing completely.

The last view Adam had, before he pulled the gate to the rear alleyway closed behind him, was of the Librarian sat hunched on the floor, a look of complete confusion on his, now far more human-looking, face.

* * *

"Right," said Charlie, as they both sat on the floor of Adam's room ten minutes later, "I think that it's time to explain what on earth just happened."

It had been a few minutes before he had been able to say anything at all, having spent the first moments back in the house pacing up and down with his head in his hands. Eventually he had calmed enough to sit down and had, initially fairly angrily, demanded some answers from Adam.

Adam paused for a moment, wondering where it was best to begin his explanation, and aware that wherever he did choose to start, nothing seemed likely to make much sense.

"Like I said earlier, it all started when my mum went missing," he began, then paused again. "You'll think I'm crazy when I tell you."

"I've just been chased across town by a psycho librarian who had some sort of weird black stuff coming out of him and could apparently freeze time," Charlie replied, his expression still slightly dazed, "you will have to do pretty well to top that for crazy!"

"Fair enough," Adam admitted, looking suitably abashed, and continued with his explanation.

"Every time I go to sleep recently, I have really strange dreams."

Charlie nodded, waiting for Adam to tell him more.

"I mean, extremely strange, it's like they're real. Every time I dream about the same place, a world of dreams where they recognise me, where they talk about my mum..." He trailed off for a moment before continuing, "...that's where I got the bag that I threw into the fire in the café." He looked back up at his friend, expecting a look of disbelief. Instead, Charlie was sat there wide-eyed, listening intently to everything that Adam was saying.

"You don't think I'm talking rubbish?" asked Adam in astonishment.

Charlie managed a weak grin, "I always think you talk rubbish," he replied, "but either I am going crazy too, or something very, very odd is going on."

"Besides," he continued, "while that Librarian freak was pretty horrible, there was some good news if you think about it."

Adam raised his eyebrow quizzically at this, "How could anything that has happened possibly be good news?"

"He was asking where your mum was," Charlie explained, "which means that he didn't know... and that could mean that she is okay."

It took a minute for what Charlie had just said to him to sink in. In the rush of escaping from the Librarian he hadn't stopped to think what it all meant, but Charlie was right. Presuming that the Librarian, or whatever Nightmare had been hiding inside him, was responsible for what had happened at Adam's house, then it meant that it hadn't managed to find his mother, that she had managed to escape.

While it didn't really bring him closer to finding his mum, and he knew it didn't mean that she was definitely okay, for the first time in a while Adam felt the smallest spark of hope. He was also incredibly impressed that Charlie had managed to work all that out, considering what they had just gone through.

"Then there's this," Adam said, pulling the pendant out from under his t-shirt and letting it hang from its chain. "I found this in my mum's room and I am pretty sure that it's the reason for all the weird dreams." He let it swing slightly, reflecting the light from the window.

Charlie stared at the pendant, before reaching tentatively for it. "Do you mind if I have a look?" he asked. Although Adam felt fiercely protective of the pendant, after the events of the morning he felt that he owed Charlie, so a little reluctantly he handed it across.

Charlie turned it over in his hands a couple of times, running his finger across the clasp that held it closed. "Does it open?"

Adam shook his head, "I've tried, but it just won't shift. I think it might be rusted closed."

"Weird," said Charlie slowly, continuing to turn the pendant over in his hand, "is it just me or does it feel a bit warm?"

Adam nodded at this, "it does feel warm sometimes... and in the alleyway earlier it seemed to get really hot just before it made that bright glow."

He held out his hand and Charlie passed back the pendant to him with a wistful look on his face. "So tonight, when you go to bed, do you think that you will dream about that place you were talking about again?"

"I don't know, I think so, or at least I hope so," Adam replied. "I know it sounds crazy, but I think that whatever has happened to my mum is connected to it."

For the moment he decided not to try and explain to Charlie about everything else going on in the dream world, about the Horror and the Nightmares. He felt he had already dealt with quite enough surprises and difficult explanations for one day.

It was with obvious disappointment that Charlie said good-night to Adam that evening before heading off to his room. Adam had explained to him earlier that he had no idea how exactly he got into the dream world when he slept, dashing Charlie's rather optimistic hopes of somehow joining him. Instead, Adam had promised to let Charlie know about everything that had happened when they got up in the morning before school.

Unfortunately, as is always the case when you really, really want to get to sleep, that night Adam found falling asleep almost impossible. He was desperate to re-enter the dream world, to see Lucid, Grimble and the others and to tell them about the close encounter with the Librarian, and if he could, to try and find out more about his mum.

He tried emptying his mind, counting to one hundred, even counting sheep (which he didn't believe actually worked but had seen plenty of times on the television), but nothing seemed to help. Instead, he lay there staring at the ceiling as the night stretched out into the early morning. As he got increasingly tired the thoughts running through his head became more and more jumbled, jumping between thinking about the cold voice that had come out of the Librarian's mouth, the unbelievable abilities that Lucid had introduced him to the night before, and the Horror that Grimble and the others had been discussing so urgently.

Despite all these fantastical thoughts, the main image that his brain kept returning to was the photo from the paper that Charlie had found and the accompanying, upsetting realisation that his mother had not been honest with him. Finally, just as he had decided that he wasn't going to get to sleep, resigning himself to a night empty of adventure and a day of being extremely tired at school, exhaustion caught up with him and he dropped away, once again, into dreams.

CHAPTER 8

It was no surprise to him this time when he awoke in the dream world. He was however extremely surprised to find himself back in the conservatory of the ancient mansion, lying on a large and slightly itchy rug in the centre of the room, rather than the clearing where he had always previously awoken.

"Excellent, most excellent... it worked," Adam heard Lucid say enthusiastically as he blinked a few times to clear his vision. Lucid was directly in front him, standing between the squat, glowering Grimble and the taller, ethereal figure of the Lady.

"We thought that we might be able to bring you directly here with the right assistance," Lucid explained, noting the rather obvious look of confusion on Adam's face. "The Lady was watching out for your return."

The Lady didn't say anything to this, although she tilted her head in acknowledgment as Lucid continued. "To our good fortune she was able to recognise you as you entered Reverie and make sure that you awoke here. We thought it would be best to bring you straight here, as things have become a little more... lively outside the City."

Adam nodded, although at the back of his mind he couldn't help but think the whole thing made him sound a bit like a fish on a hook being reeled in. While Lucid explained that they had business to attend to outside of the house, it was also immediately obvious that he too had news to share. Lucid therefore suggested they update each other as they walked, encouraging Adam to share his news first.

He quickly filled in the assembled members of the Five on what had taken place the previous day, Grimble drawing a sharp intake of breath between clenched teeth at the mention of the Librarian that had pursued them and the realisation that it was another of the Incubo. While he didn't immediately make any comment Adam could see his hands clenching and unclenching stiffly at his sides and there was a definite tightness in his movements as the group made their way back through the house.

In return, Lucid gave Adam a quick summary of their news, none of it proving to be good. The Horror had grown considerably and now, rather than simply being the subject of whispered half-rumour, it was widely known about. Maya had still not been in touch and Adam could tell, more from what Lucid left unsaid than anything he chose to share, that he was starting to doubt that she would ever do so. To make matters worse over the last twenty-four hours there had been several incidences of Nightmares much worse than normally seen both within and outside of the City.

Silent up until that point, Grimble made it clear that in his view all these things were firmly linked, that the Horror was somehow also related to the worsening of the Nightmares. As he said this he cast a sharp look at the Lady, apparently seeking some sort of reaction, although failing to receive one.

Rather than heading straight to the main entrance, Lucid led them on a brief detour to a room that looked to Adam like some sort of storybook Victorian laboratory. Although small the room was absolutely filled wall to wall with desks, shelves, and complex apparatus. It was all meticulously laid out, labelled and ordered, turning what could have been a chaotic mess into an organised and highly practical use of the limited space. The low, dark wooden desktops were filled with strangely shaped glass beakers and vials and the walls were decked with shelf after shelf stacked high with carefully marked ingredients.

From Grimble's comfortable familiarity with the room and its contents, Adam presumed that this was very much his domain. The others stood carefully to one side as he worked his way busily around, occasionally muttering half-heard depreciations or making minor adjustments when he saw a vial or beaker slightly out of place. After rummaging around in a couple of drawers and spending a few minutes decanting the ingredients, Grimble handed Adam several more of the small bags of the herbs that he had used the previous day. When he offered his thanks Grimble just flapped his hands dismissively and hurried them back out of the room, obviously uneasy with so many people filling his small laboratory.

To Adam's secret disappointment it appeared that this was to be their only stop within the house, his hopes of another chance to savour Mrs. Snug's delicious food dashed as they walked straight past the kitchen and continued towards the hallway and main entrance without stopping. Even if there hadn't been any snacks on offer, he would have welcomed the opportunity to see her anyway, just to break the increasingly strained mood he could feel as they walked.

Lucid, who was normally so chatty, was walking ahead, having hardly spoken a word after their initial exchange. It also seemed like Grimble and the Lady had fallen out, having pretty much ignored each other since Adam's arrival. Although there had been a few pointed looks, which Grimble's face was especially well suited to.

As they walked down the final long corridor leading to the main entrance Adam found himself lagging behind Grimble and Lucid and instead fell into step with the Lady, who was following quietly a few paces behind. Slightly embarrassed by his memories of the last time he had seen her, as he hovered out of control by her window, flapping his arms like a giant ungainly sparrow, Adam struggled for a suitable topic of conversation. While lots of options were bouncing around in his head it was, perhaps unsurprisingly, difficult to decide what a strangely glowing being made of pure dreams might want to talk about.

"Um... so how did you find me when I entered Reverie this time?" he eventually asked, genuinely interested in what the answer could be.

The Lady turned her head and Adam could feel her sharp blue eyes studying his face for a moment before she answered.

"I can feel the dreams of others," she replied in her strange, layered speech. "I don't know why, although Grimble suspects that it is because I come from dreams myself." Although the complexity of her voice made it hard to tell, Adam thought he could sense an undercurrent of sadness hidden within her words.

"Your thoughts are particularly strong, and I could spot you easily amongst the mass of little dreams."

Adam was strangely proud of this, although he also felt a little uncomfortable about the dismissive way that she referred to "little dreams." However, before he got the chance to continue the conversation they arrived at the main hallway and the opportunity for any further discussion passed.

At the front door they said their goodbyes to the Lady, who was staying at the house for the moment, although it seemed that she would be meeting with them later. This left Grimble and Lucid to accompany Adam through the gardens and back into the City.

"So where are we going?" Adam managed between breaths, struggling to keep up with the other two, despite Grimble's comparatively short stride. "You seem to be in a hurry."

"Unfortunately we are," Grimble told him gruffly, cutting off any further conversation, "things have become rather urgent, so less talking and more walking."

As they continued to make their way quickly down the street, in a renewed silence that was feeling increasingly awkward, Adam could see signs of the changes that Lucid had referred to earlier. On two occasions he saw sleeping dreamers being chased by their Nightmares, each time the Nightmares being noticeably larger than any he had previously seen. In both cases the nightmare creatures also seemed to be less defined than he was used to, patches of swirling darkness in the place of missing limbs or patches of skin. This was also drawing the attention of other passers-by, who Adam could see were looking at the passing Nightmares with suspicion and even fear, rather than the normal disinterest.

Although he wanted to ask more about these it was clear that he wouldn't currently get any answers from either Lucid or Grimble, so for the moment Adam had to keep his questions to himself.

After a few minutes they found themselves back at the open Market, although it seemed less densely populated than the last time Adam had visited. There were still a number of stalls and traders, but these were spread more thinly across the square, and as they walked across it the cries of the traders seemed quieter and more subdued than Adam remembered. As they reached the far side Lucid and Grimble drew to a halt and turned to face each other.

"I will see you at noon at the docks then," said Lucid. Grimble responded with a curt nod to them both, simply growling "Don't be late," before striding off in the opposite direction without a backward glance.

After they split from Grimble, Lucid seemed to relax slightly, although he maintained the previous pace of their journey.

"Much has happened in a short time Adam," Lucid told him as they walked, apparently wanting to take this chance to explain the change of mood that Adam had noticed. "As I explained news of the Horror is now widely spread, known across the City. While there isn't outright panic... yet, it is fair to say that the mood is nervous at best."

"So where are we going?" asked Adam. "Grimble said something about meeting at the docks?"

"And we will go there later," Lucid replied, "but for the moment we are headed to the Great Library. You may recall I mentioned it the last time you visited, but the circumstances of our visit may now be a little more urgent than I anticipated."

The street they were walking down opened onto a large paved public space, with a number of impressive-looking municipal buildings to three sides and a grand looking fountain in the centre of the square itself. The fountain was in the carved stone form of a great seated figure holding a book, jets of water spraying fan-like from the open pages. Across the square groups of children were playing, running laughing through the fine spray, feet splashing in the water that gathered around them. Although Adam could have happily stopped and watched this carefree scene for longer, Lucid headed directly for the building to the northern end of the square without pausing, Adam following in his wake. It was noticeably larger than its neighbors and fronted by a tall colonnade, the stone slightly pitted and weathered with age.

As they entered through tall wooden doors, the brightness of the day gave way to a much softer, muted green light that permeated the inside of the building, originating from low hanging lamps with coloured glass shades. The interior of the library was every bit as imposing as the outside of the building had suggested. Long dark wooden aisles of books stretched off into the distance, with a scattering of desks and low green felt stools interspersed amongst them. Although it was busy, the sheer size of the room meant that there remained an incredible sense of openness and space.

As they started to make their way across the floor Lucid was greeted almost immediately by a figure that Adam found unusual even for the dream world. The approaching man was taller than Lucid, but in direct contrast to Lucid's long and spindly limbs, he was almost completely round from top to bottom. Despite his size and apparent bulk, he walked incredibly nimbly and lightly across the room, making Adam think of a hot air balloon barely tethered to the ground. The lower half of his face was almost fully covered with a thick beard teased into a number of points, whilst his eyes were surrounded by what appeared to be a dark eyeshadow of some kind. That, in combination with his colourful and extravagantly tailored clothes, made him look like a giant and unusually cheerful pantomime pirate.

"Lucid, welcome," he said in a rich, resonant voice, grasping Lucid by the shoulders and planting a kiss on each of his cheeks. "And who is your comrade?" he added turning to Adam with a friendly wink.

After disentangling himself from the embrace Lucid stepped back for a moment to make introductions, initially pointing to Adam. "Bombast, this is Adam, a visitor to Reverie," then adding, "Adam, this is Bombast, head Librarian of the Great Library and a dear friend." Bombast poked Lucid playfully at this reference, nearly knocking him over despite the apparent gentleness of the movement.

Folding his arms partway across his impressive girth, Bombast studied Adam for a moment. "Hmmm.... visitor you say," he said, "I believe that there is more to him than that." He narrowed his eyes, the surrounding darkness of the eyeshadow adding to an odd sense of depth as Adam returned his gaze. "Besides no one just visits Reverie, not conscious and wandering like this youngster." He paused and clapped his hands. "Aha! I believe that we may once again have a Daydreamer in our midst."

Looking across at Lucid's disapproving glance, Bombast immediately lifted a finger to his lips in an over-the-top shushing motion. "Apologies for my indiscretion old friend," he said, "terribly bad of me. Let me try again." Leaning in close to Lucid and Adam he repeated, "I believe we may once again have a Daydreamer in our midst." But this time he said it in a mock stage whisper, his eyes darting left and right in an overly theatrical display of suspicion and caution. Lucid sighed deeply, although Adam noticed that he was still smiling despite his apparent annoyance.

"Come with me," said Bombast, indicating a glass panelled door close to the library entrance, "perhaps we could continue our conversation in my office."

Adam realised that Bombast's description of the room as an office was something of an understatement as soon as he opened the door. Immediately dazzled by the opulent décor, he sank almost up to his ankles into a rich red deep pile carpet that was far removed from the much plainer wooden flooring of the main library building. The walls of the 'office', if you could really call it that while keeping a straight face, were lined with dark wooden panelling upon which hung a variety of extremely expensive-looking tapestries and paintings.

As Adam looked around, he realised that they all had a consistent theme. In the first, a very large knight was standing proudly over the body of a vanquished dragon, a long dark beard hanging below the visor of his helmet. In the second an intrepid, although surprisingly round, explorer was in the process of planting a flag atop a rocky outcrop at the summit of a tall mountain. The third, this time an intricately weaved tapestry, showed a herculean figure which was undoubtedly Bombast once again, this time wrestling with a Nightmare in the shape of a giant bear.

"Ah, admiring the art I see," Bombast enthused. "Every now and then I like to treat myself, stops the place from looking quite so plain."

"Please, sit, sit," he added, waving them to a padded bench running the entire length of one wall, "make yourselves comfortable."

Bombast fussed around them as they sat, Adam sinking so far into the seat's deep cushions he was afraid he would eventually be swallowed whole. Firstly, he handed out exquisitely formed chocolate treats, each one a minor, slightly sickly, sculpture in its own right, then sweet biscuits and finally small cups containing hot chocolate (which in Adam's opinion, whilst exceptional was still not quite as good as that provided by Mrs. Snugs).

"So, to what do I owe the pleasure of this visit?" Bombast asked, a sparkle in his charcoal eyes. "I know that the sheer brilliance of my company is reward in itself, but I assume that there is something more on this occasion?"

Lucid straightened, as far as he was able while still sinking into the soft cushions, and placed his cup down. "As you quite rightly identified, we have a Daydreamer amongst us once again."

Adam tried to make himself look suitably impressive at this reference, but this was rather difficult when his upper lip was stained by a large hot chocolate moustache, he had a mouth half full of sweet biscuits, and he was slowly disappearing into the seating.

"And as you also know," Lucid continued, "we face the largest, most aggressive Horror that any of us can recall. I can't help but feel that the coincidence of this is too much to ignore."

Lucid exchanged a more serious look with Bombast. "You also know pretty much everything that goes on in Reverie, so I have come to ask for your help."

By this time Bombast had taken a seat in a large chair, almost throne-like in its grandeur behind his desk. He steepled his fingers, resting his chin on them and stared back across at Lucid, the previous twinkling humour in his eyes replaced by a far more serious expression.

"I have heard plenty about this Horror," he said, still staring across at Lucid, "mainly that it is both much larger and faster moving than any previously seen." He paused, drawing a deep breath before continuing. "More important perhaps is where it is moving, if what I hear is true then it has travelled in a direct line ever since appearing, without deviation."

Lucid raised a questioning eyebrow, "And where is it heading?"

Adam looked across at Bombast as he replied, the last of the natural humour had gone from his face, for a moment the darkness around his eyes making him look incredibly tired. "If it continues on its current course... then it will reach the Stairway of Dreams within two days."

Lucid sighed deeply. "I feared as much, but I wasn't fully sure... until now." He nodded to Bombast. "Thank you old friend, much as I would love to stay and enjoy your hospitality further it seems that time is against us." Casting a regretful look at the plates of treats still sitting on Bombast's desk he climbed to his feet and indicated for Adam to do the same.

"Your colleague is down in the archives deep in research as usual," Bombast informed Lucid as they made their way back out of his office. "I presume you will need to see him before you depart."

He pointed them to a doorway at the back of the main library hall and with a final wave left them to make their own way into the basement.

As they descended the stairway into the library archives the surroundings were very different from the rest of the building, the wide aisles giving way to a maze of claustrophobic passageways created by dark wood shelves stretching from floor to ceiling. The stuffy air was still and quiet, although every now and then Adam thought he could hear the rustle of old paper somewhere in the distance.

After several minutes spent working their way through the bookcase corridors, they reached what appeared to be the very centre of the basement. It was there that they found Henry seated at a small dimly lit desk with piles of books and papers spread haphazardly across it. A small bespectacled Minotaur at the centre of a paper maze.

He looked up as they approached, his face ridged with exhaustion, although Adam also thought he could sense an underlying impression of scarcely contained excitement pushing at the very edges of his expression.

"Hello Lucid," he said, the tiredness etched on his face also apparent in his voice. "Your arrival is timely, very timely indeed. I think, no, no... I am sure I have found something, something important." He pushed a pile of papers roughly to one side of the desk with a sweep of his arm, several spilling off the side, cascading unnoticed onto the floor. Henry used the space he had just cleared to open a large and dog-eared book to a page he had previously bookmarked with a folded sheet of paper.

"I was struggling to find anything that seemed like it would aid us in dealing with this Horror, it seems to have more direction and is growing faster than any that I had been able to find a record of." He jabbed his finger at the page he had just turned to. "Then I found this, in an old historical tome that goes back several centuries. Frankly it was a long shot and I was amazed to find anything." He stabbed again at the page, despite already having their full attention.

"There is reference to a previous Horror of a similar magnitude and the implications are... exceedingly worrying. If my reading of the text is correct, I think that this previous Horror was created when someone or something deliberately fed a Nightmare, cultivated it until it became something awful." For a moment Henry stopped, as if he was so appalled by his thoughts that he found it hard to express them. You could see his Adam's apple bob as he gulped a couple of times before continuing.

"If... if that was true, and if this is also the case now, somewhere there is a poor soul stuck in a nightmare filled sleep, unable to wake up and escape, while some malevolent force feeds the nightmare and makes it grow ever stronger."

Adam's eyes were drawn to the illustration halfway up the page that Henry had pointed to, a rough pen sketch of something that looked to Adam a bit like a whirlwind but formed of something darker and more solid. Even though it was only a picture, he felt a momentary chill, an inexplicable feeling of menace radiating from the page. His mind was filled with images of ragged darkness, whipping across the world, tearing a deep groove into the earth as it made its inexorable way towards them all.

Turning away from the book and facing Adam, Henry addressed his next comment directly to him, jolting Adam out of his grim imaginings.

"I have been giving this a lot of thought ever since I found this reference. While we can try and stop, or at least slow the Horror here in Reverie, we need to find the unfortunate dreamer who is the source of it in the Waking World. The only one amongst us who can do that... who is capable of travelling between the two worlds is you, Adam."

As Henry spoke, he became increasingly animated, seeming almost feverish, far removed from the mild and studious individual that Adam had previously presumed him to be. He had pushed himself up out of his chair and was leaning forward over the desk, the light from the lantern reflected off the smooth round lenses of his glasses, turning his eyes into glowing circles of emotionless light.

"Henry, Bombast has confirmed that the Horror is heading towards the Stairway," Lucid cut in. "Even if we can find the source of these troubles somewhere in the Waking World, we still need to get to the Stairway as soon as we can. I dread to think what will happen if the Horror reaches it."

He turned to Adam, "If what Henry says is true, you are likely the only one who can move between both worlds. Are you willing to help us and try to find the source of the Horror in your world... if you can?"

Adam gulped, the implications of what Henry and now Lucid were so suddenly asking him to do were pretty hard to handle. Suddenly the excitement of entering the dreamworld and the hopes of finding out more about his mother had been replaced by being responsible for the whole world.

In the past he hadn't even been allowed to take the school hamster home, as the teacher hadn't been sure that Adam could be depended upon to look after it and bring it back in one piece, but despite his worry, it was also clear that there was little alternative to what they were suggesting. Whether he liked it or not, at the back of his mind there was a tickling sensation which nagged at him, a feeling that he had a responsibility towards this place and his new group of friends that he couldn't avoid.

"I'll help if I can," he replied, a little hesitantly, "but I have no idea where to start, where to look... and it doesn't really sound as if we have very much time."

Lucid grasped him by the shoulder. "You are a brave soul Adam and we appreciate your help. We will all do our best to give you direction when you return to the Waking World."

"And if you can't?"

"Then we can only hope that the Dreamer will guide us all," replied Lucid, with a certainty in his voice that didn't quite manage to make it onto his face, which remained troubled and drawn.

He turned back to Henry.

"I have arranged to meet the others at the docks by midday," he told him. "Following Bombast's confirmation of the direction of the Horror and your further news it appears that we must depart for the Stairway immediately. I presume you will also meet us there?"

Henry looked around at the comforting surroundings of the library archives and paused for a moment before slowly nodding. "I will... I'll just gather a few things, papers and charts that might be helpful, and then I'll follow you down there."

"Very well," Lucid replied, turning to leave, "make haste though, it seems we have no time to spare."

With that he motioned to Adam to follow him once again, weaving their way back through shelves, leaving Henry looking slightly lost in the midst of his books.

CHAPTER 9

As they walked out of the library, drawing a final flamboyant wave from Bombast as they passed his office, Adam asked Lucid about the journey it seemed they were about to embark upon.

"As we have found this morning, and as we all feared might be the case, the Horror is heading towards the Stairway of Dreams," Lucid began. "We absolutely cannot let it reach the end of its journey. While we don't know for sure what will happen if it reaches the Stairway itself, it is a risk we dare not take. The Stairway is the centre of our world, the basis of our creation. There is no way we can allow it to be put in danger... to be harmed."

He stopped for a moment to point across the City. "We agreed to meet at the docks, and if the need arose to depart immediately and try and intercept the Horror. Travelling by barge is the fastest way to cross Reverie and gives us the best chance of reaching the Stairway before the Horror gets there." He sped up his pace slightly, obviously impatient to reach the docks and get the real journey underway.

Travelling across Nocturne, slowly drawing closer to the Docks the grimness of Lucid's mood seemed to lift slightly, with a lightness in his steps that hadn't been apparent before. The docks themselves were a buzzing hive of activity, seemingly far less affected by the worries that had subdued the mood in much of the rest of the City. Adam stepped aside time and again as people of all shapes and sizes barged, shuffled and on one occasion wobbled past him on something close to a unicycle, carrying all kinds of fascinating looking goods. The air was thick with the smells of mysterious fragrances mixed with the sound of a dozen different languages and dialects. To Adam's mind, always receptive to thoughts of adventure and travel, it was a heady and exciting cocktail.

Following Lucid across the crowded boardwalk, Adam eventually emerged into a slightly quieter section of the docks, which seemed to be focused more on the mooring of vessels than the bustle of trade, it was also the first time he had got close enough to the edge of the docks to see exactly what the boats were actually floating on. Rather than the wide river that Adam had been expecting to see, the edge of the docks gave way to a thick, rolling mist upon which the various vessels moored at the dockside seemed to bob quite happily.

Adam turned to Lucid with a questioning look but didn't need to go any further as Lucid, without any prompting, launched into an enthusiastic explanation.

"This my friend is the Weave," he said, indicating the rolling mists. "Every dream that ever was and ever will be comes from the Weave... and eventually returns to it."

Adam looked back at the mist and thought for a moment he could see glimpses of movement within it, almost imperceptible flashes of light or colour, too short-lived to identify. Meanwhile Lucid continued to explain.

"The Weave is another great constant of our world. In the same way that great cities in your world grew up around rivers of water as centres of trade and commerce, here we grew our cities around a river of dreams, the Weave. Over time we have learnt to navigate it and travel upon it. My people, the Sornette, developed a great love for the Weave and now many make it their home."

"And some..." interjected a grumpy voice from directly behind Adam "...some consider it to be a complete and utter pain in the backside, populated largely by idiots."

"Our good friend Grimble here," continued Lucid, without missing a beat, "does not appreciate the wonder of the Weave."

Grimble snorted as he walked past Adam. "Pah! Alternatively, you could say that some sensible people, who don't have a head full of clouds, believing that the world is full of fluff, cuddles, and kittens, are of the entirely sensible view that floating around with only a plank of wood's thickness between you and a certain drop into eternity is a foolhardy way to travel."

All of this seemed to bypass Lucid completely, who was still grinning broadly.

"You made it here on time at least," Grimble continued, "which I suppose is a blessing. I believe that the others are already on board."

He pointed at a shallow hulled and brightly coloured barge moored about fifty metres further down the docks.

"Excellent," said Lucid, rubbing his hands together and striding past Grimble towards the vessel. "Adam, let me introduce you to one of the great loves of my life, this is the Dreamskipper."

Adam could hear the pride and affection in Lucid's voice as he spoke, and he immediately understood the improvement in Lucid's mood as they had reached the docks. In much the same way that the laboratory was Grimble's home territory and the library was Henry's, this was the place that Lucid obviously knew as home.

Lucid almost bounded up the narrow gangplank as he boarded the barge, causing it to wobble rather worryingly as he did so.

"Would you just look at that lanky buffoon," Grimble said despairingly to the world at large, before starting to make his own way across. He took an incredibly long time to make the short crossing, pausing every time there was the slightest movement and continuously muttering under his breath. Although Adam couldn't make out everything that Grimble was saying, the few snippets he did pick out were not at all polite.

When he finally reached the deck and had grabbed, white-knuckled, onto the sides of the barge, Grimble turned back to Adam.

"Bear in mind that no one knows if there is a bottom to the Weave," he informed him with a grim smile. "If you were to fall in, which the occasional accident-prone idiot has done, you may well never stop falling," and with that reassuring piece of news, he turned and made his way towards the back of the barge.

This left Adam as the last to cross, deciding to look straight ahead and not think too much about what Grimble had just told him. None the less he felt very relieved when he reached the relative stability of the deck.

At the back of the barge he could see Lucid and Grimble along with the Lady, stood grouped in animated discussion around a large chart that Lucid was holding stretched open between them. To his surprise Henry was also standing there, having somehow got from the Library to the docks before them.

"So then..." he heard Lucid say as he drew closer to the group "...if we make good progress, I believe that we can reach the Stairway well within two days."

The map they were studying made little sense to Adam with his limited knowledge of Reverie's geography, but he could make out the City of Nocturne towards the southern end of the chart and the Stairway located exactly in the centre. A spider-web of dark blue channels, presumably representing the various routes and tributaries of the Weave, radiated out from the Stairway and covered much of the map, connecting the various Cities, Towns, and Villages big enough to be marked on it.

With a final look at their route, Lucid rolled the chart back up and stowed it in a cubby hole at the back of the deck before picking up a long wooden pole and making his way to the side of the barge.

"Hold on tight," he said to the world in general, advice which only Grimble appeared to take literally, immediately grabbing onto the edge rail of the barge tightly and closing his eyes with equal vigor. With that Lucid reached across and using the wooden pole to push hard against the edge of the dock, gently floated the Dreamskipper out into the centre of the Weave.

The gangly limbs that sometimes seemed so unwieldy on land suddenly made far more sense to Adam, as Lucid moved easily around the deck. His long arms gave him greater leverage as he punted the Dreamskipper down the centre of the channel, using the lengthy pole to push off from the uneven sides of the opposing banks.

They continued in that manner for about an hour before they hit a wider stretch of the Weave. Adam was increasingly impressed at Lucid's unflagging energy, his slim limbs obviously containing far more strength than he had previously given him credit for. However, now the increased width of the channel made it impossible to effectively punt the barge along, so instead he hoisted a small sail, which allowed them to continue to make progress, although at a slightly slower speed.

"Right," said Lucid, rubbing his hands together as he made his way back from the mast to where Adam and Grimble stood looking out over the rail at the front of the barge. "We have some time before I need to take over control of the Dreamskipper again. We are travelling under wind power and Henry is in charge of the tiller for the moment."

He paused to give a jaunty wave to Henry at the other end of the vessel, who waved back rather more hesitantly before quickly putting both hands back on the tiller, a look of almost comical concentration on his face. The Lady was nowhere to be seen, Adam assuming she had decided to rest in the small cabin at the back of the barge, the gentle motion of the barge apparently making her feel sick.

"I suggest we use this time as productively as we can, specifically that we continue with your training." Lucid nodded across at Grimble as he continued, "Grimble has some thoughts about what we should try next."

At this prompt Grimble moved from Adam's side and turned to face him. "We need to move straight to something serious, after all you have already faced an Incubo." He began to pace up and down as he continued to speak. "No more time for parlour tricks or tomfoolery, you need to learn how to defend yourself here... and quickly."

"So how...?" began Adam, but was cut off as Grimble continued.

"This time there is no remembering happy dreams or cheerful memories, I need you to think of things that make you angry... really, really angry."

Adam looked across and could see Grimble continuing to pace as he walked, looking angry enough for the both of them.

Taking Grimble's advice, Adam moved to the centre of the deck, closed his eyes and tried to summon up feelings of anger, to focus on thoughts that frustrated or annoyed him. Slowly the calmer atmosphere of the barge's gentle progress along the Weave was expelled from his mind as his thoughts turned inwards. Various images flashed through his mind as he tried to find the anger that Grimble was looking for, the Shop Assistant's darkness infused eyes, the chase with the Librarian, the feeling of helplessness when he had been frozen in place, but none of these seemed to generate the strength of feeling he needed.

"It's not working," he said, although keeping his eyes closed.

"Keep trying," he heard Grimble reply. "There will be something in your mind that will do the job if you dig deep enough."

Concentrating again, his mind went back to the memory of his return home on the day his mum had gone missing, the wreckage of his home, the ruin of his mother's room, and with that thought he could feel his blood start to boil. Although he had tried to put these memories to the back of his mind over the last few days, when he looked for them they were all still sitting there in his head in as much bright, miserable detail as they had ever been.

As his anger intensified, he could feel a corresponding warmth growing in his chest. Opening his eyes and looking down, he could see that the feeling was matched by a pulsing glow of light from the pendant hanging around his neck. As the fury he was feeling continued to grow, now with a life that seemed to be all of its own, the glow from the pendant worked its way down his arms and began circling his hands.

The wonder that he had initially felt was ebbing away by this point, starting to be replaced with worry. The glow was now painfully bright, and the heat of the pendant was starting to become uncomfortable.

"What do I do?" he tried to shout across to Grimble and Lucid, who were both stood watching him open-mouthed. Adam also noticed, even in his current panicked state, that they both appeared to be slowly backing away from him. Grimble mouthed something but Adam was unable to make it out over the increasing loud humming sound that now surrounded him. He squeezed his eyes partly closed and tried harder to focus on what Grimble was saying, swallowing down his panic. "Clap," he thought he made out, and while it didn't make much sense to him, in the absence of any other options, he decided to give it a try.

It was increasingly difficult to move in the middle of the storm of glowing light still localised around the pendant, but Adam managed to gradually bring his hands together. As his fingertips drew close to each other the glow that surrounded them began to arc from hand to hand and the difficulty of his movement intensified even further, but gritting his teeth he continued to force his hands together. Although to Adam it seemed as if his hands had hardly touched, the sound of the resulting clap reverberated across the deck of the Dreamskipper blasting Lucid and Grimble from their feet and creating a whirlwind of dust and debris. The shockwave also sent Adam tumbling back in the opposite direction, for one uncertain moment leaving him with the unpleasant feeling he was going to fall straight over the side, before he thankfully ground to a halt.

When the swirling dust settled and the thumping sound in Adam's ears calmed, he looked around in shock. The wooden planks of the deck that surrounded him were scorched and gently smoking, while the small sail hanging from the mast had been reduced to a few strips of ragged material. Lucid was slowly rising to his feet from where he lay several metres away, looking disorientated, and Grimble was nowhere to be seen.

"Grimble!" Lucid shouted as he wobbled rather shakily across the deck, soon joined by Adam who alternately looked around the deck and stared down at his hands in a mix of wonder and horror at what he had just done. A moaning sound from the centre of the barge caught their attention and he and Lucid made their way across to a tumbled heap of crates and barrels which had been knocked down in the blast. Looking more closely Adam could see a foot poking out from the pile. Moving several of the crates to one side revealed the prone figure of Grimble lying on his back with wisps of smoke trailing into the air from a number of patches of singed hair on his face.

"I think," said Grimble, as they helped him unsteadily to his feet, "that is probably enough training for now."

CHAPTER 10

Fortunately, while impressive, the damage Adam had inadvertently caused the Dreamskipper was largely superficial. Within an hour the sail had been replaced and they were able to continue their journey. Both Henry and the Lady, who had emerged back onto deck following the disturbance, remained at the back of the Barge staying clear of Adam and the other two. Several times Adam caught the Lady looking at him with an expression of open curiosity, while Henry just looked even more nervous than normal.

Their continuing journey took them past several small settlements and what appeared to be the local equivalent of watermills, with long, slender fins turned by the slowly flowing mist of the Weave. They had just passed one of these odd-looking constructions when another building set further back from the banks of the Weave caught Adam's attention.

A low stone boundary wall was visible through the trees, behind which you could just about make out the remains of a red-tiled roof. The building seemed large, stretching back further than Adam could see from his vantage point on the barge deck, but also completely derelict. Much of the roof was missing with plants growing through the gaps in the tiles and spreading enthusiastically across the remaining sections. The stone walls were similarly run-down, with large areas of the surviving wall scarred and stained by what looked from this distance to be the remnants of fire damage.

Although it was very clear that the fire had long since died away and the building was several hundred metres away, for the briefest of moments Adam could have sworn he could smell the scorch of flames against the stone walls and hear tiles cracking in the heat.

His concentration was broken by the touch of a hand on his shoulder.

"As I suspected we won't reach the site of the Stairway today," said Lucid stepping to one side of Adam and joining him in staring out over the Weave "but we should be able to stop overnight in a couple of miles. There is an Assembly just downstream from where we are now."

"An Assembly?"

Adam had not heard the term before, or at least not outside of the morning presentations by Mr. Stark at school. He strongly suspected that Lucid might be talking about something rather different.

"An Assembly is a gathering of my people, the Sornette," Lucid explained. "By and large we are travellers, making our way around the Weave, trading between settlements and living on barges like the Dreamskipper. Although we have no towns or cities of our own, on occasion we will gather together to meet and trade goods or tales amongst ourselves... and this is referred to as an Assembly."

His eyes misted over for a moment. "More rarely there is a Grand Assembly, where we gather from every corner of Reverie, every nook, every minor tributary of the Weave. That really is a sight to behold. Since my appointment to the Five I have stayed largely within the City, but I cannot deny that I miss this..." his voice trailed off as he was caught up in old memories.

Adam got his first view of the Assembly as they passed the next long snaking bend. As they cleared it the Weave opened up into an area equivalent in size and shape to a small lake and moored up along the far bank was a cluster of barges, similar to the Dreamskipper. Drawing closer you could see that the barges were linked together by a makeshift network of ropes, gangplanks, and walkways, creating a small floating village. On the nearest vessel a tall figure raised its hat in welcome and waved them to a spot where they were able to tie the Dreamskipper into the temporary settlement.

A few minutes of activity later and the Dreamskipper was firmly tethered to the nearest two barges, the sail had been lowered and a wooden walkway had been put in place. As Adam went to walk across this to the next barge Lucid raised a warning hand.

"Just a moment," he told Adam, "we have to wait to be invited to join the Assembly." Then he grinned as he continued, "not that anyone is ever refused, not even Grimble, but it is a tradition."

Although Adam was impatient to see the rest of this odd, floating community, he took Lucid's advice and waited by the edge of the walkway. Fortunately, he didn't have to wait long. Less than a minute later a long-limbed figure, very similar in appearance to Lucid approached them.

"Greetings travelers," the figure said in a tuneful, feminine voice. "Welcome to our gathering, you are all welcome aboard to share all that is ours."

Lucid's smile grew broader at the sight of the figure. "Tremello," he said walking swiftly across the walkway and hugging the new arrival before stepping back with an embarrassed cough.

Turning back to Adam and the others he gestured to the figure, "Everyone, this is Tremello."

At this introduction she removed her hat, a shiny bowler with a daisy chain of flowers around the brim and nodded a greeting to each of them in turn.

"Tremello, let me introduce you to Grimble, (at which he nodded curtly and muttered something under his breath, presumably welcoming), The Lady (she inclined her head and gave a gentle smile), Henry (who blushed at the attention and stammered a barely comprehensible "hello") and Adam, traveler from the Waking World."

Having learned his lesson earlier, Adam didn't try and make any sort of heroic impression, settling instead for a wave and cheery grin.

Now they had been invited aboard the other barges, Adam couldn't wait to see the rest of the Assembly and was soon following closely behind Lucid and Tremello as they moved from boat to boat, Lucid exchanging genial greetings with everyone that he saw.

Adam quickly decided that the 'Sornette' as Lucid had named his people were;

1. Extraordinarily cheerful
2. Extremely tall
3. Prone to wearing brightly coloured clothing that gave your eyes a headache
4. Very, very fond of hats, most of which were decorated with a variety of odd adornments, trinkets, and knick-knacks

While the first impression of the Assembly itself had been of a disorganised cluster of barges randomly tied together, as they made their way deeper into the gathering, a sense of underlying organisation and functionality became more obvious. On one barge several of the Sornette were involved in a spirited haggling session, long limbs gesticulating in exaggerated expressions of surprise or disgust at the prices being discussed. On another, slightly larger vessel, a number of temporary trestle tables had been set up and food was being served, with Lucid obviously struggling to resist stopping for a quick taste. However it was the third barge, the biggest they had crossed so far, that proved to be the most interesting.

Both longer and wider than the other vessels, it seemed that this was the centre of the temporary floating community. At one end several large chairs were lined up in front of another trestle table, this time laden with various jugs and glasses, while at the other a number of the Sornette were preparing what looked like musical instruments of some sort. Looking around Adam could see several more groups crossing from the surrounding vessels and gathering around the edges of this larger barge. All of the Sornette were dressed in a similar fashion to Lucid and Tremello, the men in fancy waistcoats and jackets and the women in layers of brightly coloured skirts. Each one of them was also wearing a hat of some kind. Generally these were bowler or top hats, each decorated in a unique way. Some had flowers around the brim similar to Tremello, others had feathers, and a few had other, more unusual, additions.

At the far end, several of them were now seated at the table, with the central chair taken by an elderly Sornette woman wearing so many layers of skirts that she took up twice the space of her companions. Her hat was also the most extravagant that Adam had seen, a top hat even larger than Lucid's covered in flowers, clusters of feathers, fragments of bone and other random items including what looked like a selection of silver cutlery.

"Who is that?" asked Adam, with a nod towards the elderly woman.

"That is the Maman," Lucid informed him. "Every Assembly of the Sornette is led by one, normally the oldest woman in the clan."

As they watched, the elderly woman rose slowly to her feet.

"Welcome to you all," she began, in a surprisingly strong voice, "not only do we have the pleasure of each other's company this evening," at which there were a few light-hearted whistles and catcalls between the groups clustered around the edges of the barge, "but we also have visitors, including the return of one of our own." She gestured towards Lucid who removed his hat and bowed deeply. The Maman raised both hands into the air, "so tonight let us all celebrate."

As she concluded speaking and re-took her seat the musicians at the opposite end of the great barge immediately began to play the opening notes of a lively tune.

"It looks like we have arrived at a good time," said Lucid cheerily over the growing swell of the music, "how is your dancing Adam?"

"I don't know," replied Adam honestly. "I don't think I have really danced that much before."

"You will be fine," Tremello told him, reassuringly taking his hand, "just follow what Lucid and I do."

Lucid took his other hand and looking to his left and right Adam could see the Sornette linking hands all around the barge forming a large circle. He also caught sight of Grimble slowly backing away from the gathering with a look of absolute horror on his face, before his hands were grasped firmly by two tall Sornette Ladies, one to either side of him.

As the pace of the music slowly increased the circle began to move in time, Lucid and Tremello stepping their feet nimbly from side to side. Adam tried his best to copy them and after a few initial missteps, when he was particularly grateful for the hands holding his, he was able to roughly keep time with their movements. Once he had his feet organised he was also able to look up and concentrate more on what was going on around him. The circle of dancers was now slowly revolving its way around the edges of the barge, feet stepping and bodies twisting and turning in time with the music's rhythm.

Interspersed amongst the Sornette he could see his companions. Closest to him was the Lady, completely composed and moving perfectly in time with the music. Further around the circle, Henry was making a spirited, although rather clumsy, attempt to match the movements of the Sornette to either side, his previous shyness apparently forgotten in the magic of the moment. Finally, almost exactly opposite Adam was Grimble, still sandwiched between the two Sornette ladies, their bright skirts flashing from side to side as they danced. In contrast, Grimble trudged around heavily in his large boots, his already incredibly grumpy and resigned expression getting even more thunderous every time the edge of a flailing skirt caught him in the face.

The band continued to increase the tempo of the music, the lead musician playing an instrument that looked like an oversized violin, long limbs meaning that they were able to play across far more strings than a regular instrument. The music, whilst lively, was also full of subtle textures and the more it played the more Adam was able to stop concentrating so hard on his movements and just let the feeling of the music flow through him.

As the pace increased further two of the dancers released their grasp on each other's hands, breaking the circle and turning it instead into a long snaking line. The lead dancer then led them over the nearest walkway and the dance began to wend its way around, across and between the nearest barges, flowing alternately between barge decks and gangplanks.

His previous nerves about the precarious plank crossings forgotten, Adam let himself be led, confident in the guidance of Lucid and Tremello to either side. Soon enough they had completed their circuit and returned to the central barge where the circle reformed. Both the Lady and Henry had expressions of elation on their faces, looking like they had felt the same temporary joy and freedom that Adam had experienced as they had whirled around in the dance.

The spot in the circle where Grimble had been reluctantly press-ganged into dancing was now empty, but looking across the barge Adam spotted him shakily making his way over to an empty seat, before sitting down heavily with the determined expression of someone who wouldn't easily be parted from the chair's comfortable embrace for some time.

As the dance concluded and the musicians played a final flourish to applause and shouts of appreciation from the gathered crowd, one of the Sornette came across and tapped Tremello on the shoulder before leaning in and muttering something into her ear. She nodded once in response and turned to Adam and Lucid.

"If you are so minded the Maman would like to speak with you," she said to Adam. "If you would please follow me, and I will introduce you."

Adam looked across at Lucid who gave him a quick reassuring tilt of the head. "Go and speak with her and make sure of your manners, it is a privilege to be invited. I will be waiting here for you with the others when you are done."

Taking Adam's hand Tremello led him through the clusters of Sornette that had quickly gathered following the conclusion of the dance, chatting and laughing amongst themselves. As they cleared the last group Adam got a better view of the top table, the chairs to either side of the Maman having been vacated, leaving her seated alone. Above the seats a makeshift canopy had been formed from a mismatched set of blankets and sheets hanging over long wooden poles lashed roughly together, casting her half into shadow. As he approached she raised a hand in welcome and beckoned Adam to take the seat next to her. Tremello gave his hand a quick reassuring squeeze before leaving him to his audience and heading back towards Lucid and the others.

Adam sat down as directed, a little nervously and wondering whether he was supposed to do anything more formal when meeting someone like this. She was obviously important, perhaps he should bow or offer to shake hands... or perhaps here that would be some sort of terrible insult? However, his mind was soon put to rest when the wizened face opposite him broke into a gummy smile and one of the milky eyes closed in a wink.

"Welcome Daydreamer..." the Maman began, then laughing softly to herself continued "...oh my days indeed... to see another Daydreamer in my lifetime, what luck I have."

Her voice had an accent and an odd intonation that Adam couldn't place, but he found the lilting and slightly musical tone pleasant and easy to listen to.

He was also starting to wonder if he had a neon sign around his neck flashing the word 'Daydreamer' over and over, first Bombast and now this old woman seeming to spot what he was without hesitation. Apparently aware of his thoughts the Maman gave another throaty chuckle.

"Don't worry young thing, it takes many years of living and learning to spot one like you. Most wouldn't be having any clue at all that you are anything other than a little gawky thing."

Adam subconsciously straightened in his seat, trying to look a little less gawky, but the Maman didn't seem to notice.

"Anyway," she continued, "our Lucid wouldn't be travelling with just any little lost soul, you would have to be something especially peculiar to be joining him and his rag-tags on their journeying."

"And besides..." the Maman said, raising gnarled hands to her hat and removing a number of the knick-knacks that surrounded it before placing them on the table in front of them "... Maman has ways of knowing things and seeing things that aren't to be seen by most of us."

She indicated the random objects now spread out, a shard of bone, a silver teaspoon, a dried flower, and a small leather pouch. For a moment she took her shrewd gaze away from Adam's face and concentrated instead on the table-top, muttering to herself in a language that Adam didn't recognize and gently prodding a few of the items around until they were in a position she seemed to be satisfied with.

She looked back up at Adam. "I have knowings for you... if you want them."

Adam leant forward in his seat, letting his eyes drop for a moment to look at the odd collection of items on the table before looking back up at the Maman.

"Knowings?" he asked, not entirely sure what this meant.

"Yes indeed," the Maman replied, holding his gaze. "A life as long as mine spent on the Weave opens your mind's eye to all sorts of unexpected thinkings and understandings... and I know you have some questions in your heart that you can't seem to leave behind."

Despite his reservations, Adam nodded at this, there were certainly things that he wanted... that he needed to know.

"Very well," said the Maman, closing her eyes for a moment, and although her voice became quieter as she continued, somehow Adam could hear her more clearly than before, as if all the background noise and distraction had been filtered out. "You are a visitor to this world and yet you feel some connection to it, am I correct?"

Adam started to nod, then realising that the Maman couldn't see this as her eyes were still closed, he mumbled a hesitant "Yes," instead.

The Maman nodded contentedly, "and you have questions, unanswered questions about your past, your family, this is also true is it not?"

Again Adam had to agree. More than anything else, despite the extraordinary circumstances he found himself in, these were the questions that he could still feel eating away at him, the ones that came out to play in his head when he closed his eyes. He thought back to when all this had started, the family tree project at school and then later the realisation in the library that his mother had misled him about his past and his family. Her eyes still closed the Maman sucked a deep breath in, which made a slightly unpleasant damp whistling sound as it passed through her last few remaining teeth.

"There is a reason you feel so at home here young thing, a reason why you sometimes feel lost when you are away..."

Adam leant further forward, entirely focused now on the words of the old woman. She paused for a moment, her eyelids flickering. Then with a sudden movement she shot upright in her seat her eyes snapping open, causing Adam to pull back in surprise.

The Maman inhaled deeply once, muttering the word "Fire." Then gripping the arms of the chair, she pushed herself to her feet with surprising speed repeating "Fire!" but this time as a shout, her raised voice loud above the surrounding hubbub. Adam looked around in surprise and from around the Assembly he could hear the shout repeated, passing from voice to voice.

For a moment he couldn't see it, then as his eyes refocused, he spotted several patches of distant glowing haze from across the assembled barges that he had previously taken to be torches lit against the gathering dark of the evening. The Maman had left her chair, and with a strength that belied her apparent age and frailty, she pulled Adam to his feet and pushed him hard in the back, in the general direction of Lucid and the others.

"Go quickly... take your friends and go," she commanded and then turned and rapidly shuffled off towards the back of the grand barge shouting commands to several Sornette who had emerged from the cabin.

As Adam approached Lucid and the others he could see the confusion in their expressions, Henry's mouth hanging open in shock, Grimble's eyes widening as he spotted something over Adam's shoulder.

Unable to stop himself Adam turned to look at what had caught Grimble's attention and found himself looking back at a scene of terrible chaos. Across the great barge several patches of dark, eddying smoke, man-sized tornados of darkness, formed and then dissipated. Each time they did this they left a patch of flame burning behind them. Groups of the Sornette were already running across the deck desperately trying to smother the growing fires with dampened cloths, but it seemed unlikely to Adam that they were going to be able to keep pace with the rate at which new fires were starting.

This fact was also not lost upon Tremello, who was still stood alongside Lucid, her eyes bright and hands clenched in impotent anger at what she was seeing. Despite this she seemed to have kept her composure, and as Adam reached the group, she pointed across the barge.

"Come on, follow me now before the fire spreads to the Dreamskipper," she barked, her voice cracking with emotion.

Without pausing for any response she grabbed Lucid's hand and started to drag him towards the nearest gangplank. Adam and his companions following after them at a half run, even Grimble making the crossing at a reasonable pace. As they ran across the last barge before theirs, dodging between tables now overturned in panic, a whirlwind of darkness spun into existence almost directly in front of them. Up close Adam could see the smoky substance more clearly, looking very similar to the dark tendrils that the Nightmare Librarian had tried to use on him.

Without stopping to think Adam concentrated the mixture of emotions he was feeling, an unpleasant cocktail of fear, anger, and shock that he could feel deep in his stomach, and threw it all into his hands, thrusting them into the centre of the gathering darkness and then clapping them together as they reached its centre. As before a glowing pulse of light formed around his pendant and spread rapidly down his arms.

By the time he brought his hands together the light had already reached the tips of his fingers. This time, rather than the uncontrolled blast of his last attempt, the shockwave he created was contained within the centre of the massing patch of dark shadow, which immediately shattered like glass.

As it violently fragmented around him Adam dropped to his knees, a sudden rush of dark thoughts flooding his brain, swamping everything else completely. As the swirling darkness had splintered around him, he had felt some sort of connection. A horrible, unwanted connection, but it had been there all the same. The surrounding chaos faded into the background, and in his mind's eye he saw another dark whirlwind, but infinitely bigger than the one he had just faced, stretching so high into the sky that it blocked out the sunlight. Its edges were ragged and sharp, and wherever it travelled it carved an ugly scar deep into the ground, plants and trees rotting and withering in its wake, packs of animals running blindly to escape its awful influence.

It was terrible, but mindless, like a huge wounded beast lashing out in pain, unaware that it was hurting everything around it. But there was something else, another presence that Adam could feel, much smaller but somehow also much worse. While the huge swirling monstrosity was a mass of random energy, ripping the world around it apart, the smaller being was the opposite, prodding, taunting... directing. Then from within the darkness a pair of bright eyes appeared, looking out from the shadows and staring straight at Adam.

"No... this is mine!"

Then the vision faded, and Adam snapped back into the present, the rush of returning noise hitting him like a truck. Strong hands grabbed hold of him, lifting him by his arms and dragging him, feet trailing, across the last gangplank to the Dreamskipper. Unceremoniously dumped with his back resting against the barge's rail, still too drained to move, Adam blinked smoke out of his eyes as he tried to take in the activity going on around him.

Lucid was rapidly lowering the small central sail, while Tremello had stayed on the nearest barge frantically cutting at the ropes tethering the Dreamskipper to the surrounding vessels. Across the Assembly more fires were breaking out and Adam saw one of the farthest barges begin to fragment, sections dropping away into the depths of the Weave.

"Go, go!" shouted Tremello as she cut through the last of the connecting ropes, and grabbing hold of one of the long punting poles she started to push the Dreamskipper away, clear of the rest of the Assembly. Lucid called across to her, holding out his hand in an unspoken invitation to join them, and for the briefest of moments Adam could see she was torn by indecision. Then she turned away from the slowly drifting Dreamskipper and began instead to run back towards the nearest fire and the panicked shouts of the other Sornette.

As they began to move further away from the remaining cluster of barges Adam could see pockets of desperate activity as the Sornette tried to cut away the most badly damaged barges and douse the growing patches of fire on the others. Amongst them he thought he could make out the darting figure of Tremello and the voluminous skirts of the Maman as she moved more slowly amongst the others, shouting orders and directing their efforts.

"What was that?" panted Lucid, staring back across at the receding Assembly with wide, disbelieving eyes, his voice full of frustration at his inability to help. Several brightly burning barges had now successfully been cut loose and were drifting clear of the group, while on the remaining barges the battle to contain any new fires continued.

Finding Lucid's expression too painful to face, Adam turned instead for a moment to look at the others. The Lady was stood leaning on the side staring in dismay, her eyes full of sadness at the sight of the burning vessels. Henry was alongside her, emotions hidden by the dancing flames reflected in the lenses of his glasses. Further back he could see Grimble pacing up and down, ignoring the scene they were leaving behind, appearing to be fully caught up in thoughts of his own.

Turning back, the last view that Adam had before they passed the next bend in the Weave was the glow of fire on one of the abandoned, drifting barges. Then there was a ripple of movement on it and another of the dark whirlwinds formed. Highlighted against the orange haze for a brief moment he thought he saw the silhouette of a figure step from it, heavier set than the slim limbed Sornette. The shadowy outline lifted an arm, seeming to point towards Adam and then the flow of the Weave took them away and the figure was lost to sight.

CHAPTER 11

For what seemed to Adam like an incredibly long time, they travelled without speaking more than a couple of words to each other, all too stunned by what had just happened. Then rising from the seat he had made amongst the stacked sacks partway down the barge, Grimble broke the silence. He walked past Adam to where Lucid was standing and addressed him directly. "I am sorry for what happened to your friends… they made a great sacrifice to see us safely on our way."

Lucid didn't reply. His eyes were distant and his face was twisted in pain, haunted by the flames of the burning barges still dancing across his vision. Shrugging slightly, although with a look of gruff sympathy remaining on his face, Grimble continued.

"But we must face facts, whatever that thing was, it seems likely that it was there for us. It is more than a coincidence that as soon we left the fires appeared to diminish."

The other two had also come back across by this point, both now listening closely to Grimble's words.

"So we have to ask ourselves how it knew we were there, how it found us. No one should have been aware of what we were doing or where we were going."

Lucid's eyes had regained their focus by this point and narrowed at Grimble's latest comment.

"It is quite possible that someone could have guessed, Bombast and possibly others knew that we were headed for the Stairway."

"Perhaps, or perhaps not," muttered Grimble in response, although not quite under his breath, his eyes moving slowly around the group. Adam felt that he was sizing each of the companions up for a moment, testing for a weak link.

"I know what you are suggesting, and I refuse to believe it," said Lucid, "none of us would endanger the others."

"So you say..." Grimble snapped back "...but remember we have been betrayed by one of our own before."

Casting a now openly hostile look back at them Grimble stalked away, although only as far as the other end of the barge, where he sank heavily to the floor, resting his head in his hands.

"Well, that was beyond... I mean that was not at all, I am really not very happy..." began Henry, removing his glasses and beginning to angrily rub at them with a small square of cloth, but the Lady interrupted him with a gentle touch to his arm.

"His past experiences have made him doubtful and we have all been through something that is difficult to deal with. His mood will lighten and he will realise his error."

Henry, still looking aggrieved, nodded slightly. "Fine... fine, you are right I am sure, we are all a bit... you know..." His sentence stuttered into silence and he made a rather limp and hopeless gesture, as if this explained his remaining unspoken thoughts.

Although he felt guilty for even entertaining the thought Adam found himself, just for a moment, looking at Henry's face rather than his gesticulating hands, checking for any hints of darkness in his eyes before he replaced his glasses. Then he shook the thought from his head, determined that he would not let Grimble's apparent paranoia rub off on him any further.

The next hour passed in uncomfortable silence. Despite the Lady's calming words Henry would occasionally shoot hurt looks in Grimble's direction, while the Lady, after several failed attempts to start a conversation with either Lucid or Grimble, had eventually returned once again to the small cabin.

Adam had decided to keep his distance and had taken a spot at the very front of the barge, and because of this he was the first to spot the change in the Weave. A few hundred metres in front of them the glow of the Weave seemed to intensify and a soft bank of mist began to rise from it, which eddied around the bow of the Dreamskipper as they drew close, making it increasingly hard to see far ahead. Adam shouted back to the others and Lucid slowed the progress of the barge in response, lowering the small sail.

Then emerging from out of the mist, which continued to softly snake up from the gently eddying surface, Adam spotted a small bottle floating towards them. As it drew close and passed by the side of the Dreamskipper he could see a tightly rolled sheet of paper poking from the top.

"Is that... a message in a bottle?" he asked in disbelief, pointing it out to Lucid.

"I don't know," Lucid replied, "I have never seen such a thing before. Wait a moment."

Lucid made his way to the back of the Dreamskipper and returned with a net on the end of a long pole, but to Adam's disappointment the bottle had passed them by this point and all he could do was helplessly watch it bob gently into the distance. The noise had also caught the attention of the others and for a moment the temporary dispute that had split them was forgotten as they all watched the odd little bottle floating away.

Turning to face the front of the barge again, Adam's eye was caught by a glint of light in the distance, which as it drew closer proved to be another bottle reflecting the lantern hanging from the barge's bow. Then to Adam's amazement he saw another following just behind it, then another... and another. Within a few moments the Weave was filled with pinpricks of reflected light as tens and then hundreds of bottles, almost covering the surface of the Weave, floated towards them. For a minute they all stood transfixed, staring in wonder at the sight in front of them, the Weave temporarily turned into a constellation of small, glowing stars. Then, remembering himself, Lucid lowered the net, snagging one of the bottles and lifted it back onto the deck.

He leant down and picked up the bottle, gently pulling the paper from the bottle's neck with his slim fingers and unrolling it. After looking down for a moment he called Adam across.

"I believe that this is meant for you," he said softly.

Adam gingerly held the paper out and began to read, pausing for a heart-stopping moment as he recognised his mother's unmistakable small, neat handwriting, before continuing.

"My brave, wonderful boy, I hope this message reaches you and more than that, that you can understand and forgive me for everything that has happened. I have wanted to contact you, to speak to you, to see you again, but I have not had the strength until now. I know that Lucid will have taken good care of you, have kept you as safe as he can, keeping his promise to me. I knew that this day would come, that the dreams of my past would come back to haunt me... and that it would put you in danger too. I have tried to prepare you as well as I could, to make you as strong and as ready as you could be, to prepare you for the dream world and all that you may have to face."

Adam stopped reading for a moment, his mind temporarily overwhelmed. The thought repeating over and over in his brain was that his mother was alive and out there somewhere, and more than that, somehow she had found him here, in Reverie, and was thinking of him. By comparison, the unbelievable way in which she had contacted him faded into insignificance, remarkable as it was.

As he re-read the first paragraph of the letter he thought back over the life he and his mother shared, the stories that had inspired nightly dreams of adventure and her insistence the last time they had spoken that dreams and imagination were the most important gifts he had.

With these thoughts still orbiting his brain he realised with a sudden clarity that everything that his mother had done for him, every story, had been far more than made up tales, more than imagined adventures. They all had a purpose much deeper than he had ever realised, preparation for this moment, making his ability to dream stronger.

It was a strange realization to come to, and he was pretty sure that not many people would be able to relate to the odd mix of feelings flooding through him, but nevertheless when he looked down to read the concluding section of the letter it was with a new sense of purpose.

"*You will have realised by now that something terrible is happening. Something that I tried and failed to stop. I hate to put you in any kind of danger, but it seems it is too late for that, so now I must ask you to do something incredibly important and much as I hate to admit it even to myself, there is no one else who can do what you can.*"

Adam's eyes widened as he read the next short sentence, the last in the letter, just four words long. The words were written slightly larger and more uneven than the preceding paragraphs, as if emphasising the urgency that the writer was trying to express.

"*You must save Nora!*"

CHAPTER 12

Lucid, Grimble, Henry and the Lady looked back across at Adam, a mix of excitement and puzzlement on their faces. Adam had just finished describing the content of the letter to them, and while they had allowed him to complete his description without interrupting, it was only a matter of a few further moments before Henry asked the first question.

"So who is Nora... and why would she need saving?"

"I don't really know her," Adam replied honestly. "She is just a girl that started at my school, just before everything went wrong."

The rate of his explanation slowed as he started to think more about the implications of what he was saying. "It was the day before my mum went missing and then... then she stopped coming into school, they said that she had become very ill all of a sudden."

As he finished speaking, he could see the meaningful looks being passed between the others. Grimble coughed awkwardly and leant forward.

"She could be the one Adam," he said. "If what Henry found in the Library is true then she could be the source of the Horror, the unfortunate one stuck in a permanent bad dream."

Lucid continued where Grimble had left off. "Why else would your Mother say she needs saving? It's too much of a coincidence to ignore. Or if nothing else a possibility that we must consider."

Adam nodded hesitantly. "I don't even know where she is now, but I can try and find out what happened to her, if you really think that would help."

Lucid smiled reassuringly and grasped Adam by the shoulder, bending at the knees to bring his face level with Adam's.

"I am sure it will help Adam, besides which you have been through a great deal in the last day and will have to return to the waking world again soon. Now we have a lead to follow, a source of hope." He glanced for a moment across at the glass bottle which had carried Adam's mother's message, "no matter how strange the means by which we received this particular clue."

At the mention of the need to return to the Waking World, Adam found himself stifling a yawn, Lucid's reminder triggering the feelings of tiredness that Adam had been suppressing until that point. But rather than giving in to the fatigue that he could feel starting to ache in his muscles and weighing down his eyelids he shook himself, still having questions of his own he wanted answering while he had the chance.

"What does this mean?" he asked, adding, "I don't mean what my mother said about saving Nora, but how did she contact me, how did she do all this?" indicating the bottle and then holding up the message.

"Where is she, is she here in Reverie?" He slumped as the energy went out of his voice. "I just want to see her."

Rather than answering Adam directly Lucid looked across at Grimble.

"Your mother was a great Daydreamer Adam," Grimble began, "and she could make extraordinary things happen. Here on the Weave you are as close to the source of all dreams as it is possible to be, so perhaps, wherever your mother might be, this is where she found it easiest to reach you."

"But sadly," Lucid added, when it became obvious that Grimble had finished what he had to say, "it doesn't give us any real clue to where your mother is, other than to believe that she is currently somewhere within Reverie. I am sorry Adam, I truly am, but we can't tell you any more than that."

Adam sighed and then nodded in resignation. "I just hoped that she might be near, that I might be able to see her again."

Grimble leant forward and awkwardly patted Adam on the

head, his rough hands flattening down Adam's hair. "I understand, but try and draw some comfort from the fact that she is alive and well. When this is done we will help you find her, I promise you."

"What will you do while I'm gone?" asked Adam as he yawned again, more widely this time.

"We will continue on to the Stairway and prepare as well as we can," replied Grimble. "In the past we have been able to use the Weave itself. Although it takes some time, the dreams it contains can counteract the nightmares that form the core of the Horror. To do that we will need to divert the direction of some of its flow, and that," he added, "will require both hard labour and time," indicating a pile of tools stacked on the deck.

"So let's hope that we are all successful in our various ventures," said Lucid, a slight smile returning to the edges of his mouth for the first time in a while. "Good luck back in your world."

"Good luck to you too," Adam replied, reaching out and taking Lucid's long-fingered hand in his before shaking it firmly. He yawned again and sat down on the deck, his eyes now impossibly heavy, finding a section of sacking that looked fairly comfortable and balling it into a makeshift pillow. A few moments after his head touched it, despite the rough, slightly scratchy texture, his eyes closed and he dropped away.

CHAPTER 13

Adam's eyes snapped open, once again taking in the familiar surroundings of Charlie's spare room. But this time, rather than spending any time lying in bed and mulling over the events of the previous night, he was up and getting himself dressed within seconds, his head still reverberating with the last words in his Mother's letter. "You must save Nora!"

He ran downstairs for his breakfast, taking the stairs two at a time and nearly tumbling down the last couple as a result. When he got to the kitchen Charlie was already there waiting for him, eyes wide and keen for news of the night before. As soon as he saw Adam, Charlie jumped to his feet.

"How did it go..." Charlie began, then paused. "Wow... you look pretty awful, what happened?"

Although he didn't really want to go over it all, Adam tried to summarise everything that had taken place during the night. It ended up taking much longer than he first thought, as he quickly realised he would need to explain the Horror and a lot of the other things he had kept to himself the last time he had spoken to Charlie. Despite this, he had just managed to reach the end of his explanation, with Charlie's eyes widening even further at the final reference to Nora, when Charlie's parents came into the kitchen and the boys had to stop their discussion.

For the remainder of breakfast they sat opposite each other unable to continue their conversation, although every time Adam would look up from his bowl of cereal he would see Charlie wiggling his eyebrows in what he presumably thought was a meaningful yet subtle way.

"Are you all right Charlie?" asked his dad, peering at them

from above his morning paper.

"Fine… absolutely fine, fine and um… completely normal, why?" replied Charlie, which to Adam sounded about the most suspicious and unconvincing thing he had ever heard.

"It's just your face keeps on twitching rather oddly," said his dad, "I wondered if you were feeling okay?"

"I'm fine thanks," Charlie repeated, rather awkwardly, and quickly went back to concentrating on his breakfast, keeping from making eye contact with Adam for the rest of their meal.

✳ ✳ ✳

By the time they left the house and started on the short walk to school a few minutes later, Charlie was almost exploding with the frustration of holding in his questions.

"What on earth do you mean, you have to save Nora?" asked Charlie. "It's all a bit odd isn't it, your mum getting in touch with you… which is great news by the way. But then there's all this about Nora?"

"I don't exactly know," Adam told his friend. "I'm not used to all this either. Most people just get a phone call, or maybe an email or letter… seems like it's just me that gets weird floaty dream bottles. I just know what I told you, that Nora is supposed to be in some kind of terrible trouble and that whatever is happening to her is affecting the dream world I have been telling you about."

"Look," said Charlie, appearing to come to some sort of decision within himself, "I think I might know where Nora could be, I heard my mum talking to her parents on the phone yesterday. They mentioned something about St. Alfred's Hospital, I think that might be where she has been taken. They were talking about the local hospital not having the facilities they needed for her."

Charlie paused for a moment, then sighed. "If you really need to find her, that is probably your best chance, and from the sound of it you don't have any time to lose." He took another pause and breathed in deeply for a moment. "But that means that we have to go there right now... and that means missing school."

Adam looked across at his friend open-mouthed in surprise. Charlie who had never been in trouble, never had a detention, now talking about skipping school for the day.

They had nearly reached the street with their school and Adam realised that they would have to make the decision now. He grabbed Charlie by the elbow and pulled him up.

"Look, Charlie," he said, "I really appreciate what you're doing, but think about the choice you are talking about."

He pointed for a moment to the road in front of them. "If we turn left, we can carry on to school and try our best to have a normal day, we go to our classes, pick up our homework, and if we are lucky stay out of trouble with Miss. Grudge. If we turn right, then we are absolutely guaranteed to get into a world full of trouble. We will probably be grounded and be put in detention for at least a year. And this is all based on a message from my mysteriously vanished mum that I can't show you because I got it in an imaginary bottle, floating on a river of dreams, in a dream world that you have never seen."

Charlie looked across at him incredulously. "Well seeing as how you put it like that," he grinned, "obviously we have to turn right."

With a wide smile he shook his arm free of Adam's grasp, and without waiting for Adam to say anything else, started on the road that led away from the school and towards the bus station.

❊ ❊ ❊

St. Alfred's was a large Victorian brick building, surrounded by less grand prefabricated mobiles and extensions, rather clumsily bolted onto the original construction. It was right on the outskirts of the next nearest town, taking Adam and Charlie about thirty minutes to reach on the bus. They had spent their time on the bus journey looking up details of the hospital on Charlie's phone and had packed their blazers and ties into their rucksacks to try and look slightly less conspicuous. Fortunately, the bus stop was directly outside the main entrance to the hospital, and this early in the morning most of the people walking in and out looked like they were staff, although there was also a handful of patients with early appointments.

Charlie nodded up at the blue signs just outside the entrance listing out the main hospital wards. "If she is here, she will be in the Malcolm Smith Ward. I think that's where it said the children's section was."

"What are we going to do now though?" asked Adam. "We're not members of her family and I don't think that it's visiting hours anyway."

Charlie paused in thought for a moment and then strode towards the entrance before turning back around and beckoning to Adam.

"Just follow me and look confident," he said, walking through the door and straight past the reception desk. Without stopping to think about it too much Adam followed him, trying his hardest to look like someone who was definitely supposed to be there, exactly the same as all the other patients and their accompanying families and friends milling around in the reception area. Some were finding seats to pass the time while they waited for their name to be called, while others clustered around the entrance standing on tiptoes as they tried to get a mobile phone signal.

"Look," said Charlie pointing out the directional signs on the wall of the nearest corridor, one of which was for the Malcolm Smith Ward. Whistling nonchalantly, and as result immediately drawing questioning stares from several passers-by, Charlie made his way down the corridor with Adam following closely behind him feeling incredibly conspicuous.

As they reached the end of the hallway, he could see an obvious change in the decoration of the corridor to their left. In contrast to the institutional green of the previous walls, these were painted a yellowish colour. Adam presumed it had originally been a cheerful and sunny shade, but it now looked rather worn and sorry for itself. The walls were also partially covered in posters and paintings which had been produced by children, many also signed in large scrawling text. A scene showing a windmill in the middle of an open field immediately to Adam's side had been signed by Milly, age 6½, making the more easily distracted part of Adam's brain wonder at what point it was no longer appropriate to include your age when signing pieces of artwork.

"This way," hissed Charlie in a hushed voice, despite there being no one else in the corridor with them, focusing Adam's attention back onto the matter in hand. He walked across to the first of the doors running down the corridor, peering through the doorway before heading back to Adam and shaking his head.

"Well she's not in that one," he said. "There are quite a few rooms to check and sooner or later someone is going to spot us, so maybe it would be faster if we split the rooms between us."

Agreeing that this was the most sensible plan Adam made his way to the next room on the left-hand side of the corridor while Charlie checked the room opposite. They continued like this for several minutes, alternating rooms between them, although none of those they checked proved to contain Nora. This left one final room at the far end of the corridor, which unlike the others had its door firmly closed and a blind pulled down over the glass window panel.

"What do you reckon," said Adam, "it's going to be a lot harder explaining ourselves if we go into a closed-up room and someone catches us."

"I say we go for it," replied Charlie excitedly. "I mean we have come all this way and we're going to be in trouble anyway, so we might as well make sure we have checked everywhere."

Adam looked at Charlie, who he could see was obviously nervous despite his determined words, and once again counted himself lucky to have such a good friend to rely on, even when things got really, really weird.

"You check the room and I'll keep watch," said Charlie seriously, "if I see anyone coming I will make a noise like an owl to warn you."

Despite himself, Adam let a chuckle escape.

"What's so funny?" asked Charlie, stung by Adam's reaction.

"We are in the middle of a hospital and it's daytime," Adam explained, still grinning, "I don't think that anyone will believe that there's an owl flapping about somewhere nearby."

"Fine, but that's what they always do in films and it seems to work," Charlie muttered "I'll make a beeping sound or... something instead then. Just get moving before we're seen."

Knowing that Charlie was right, and doubting they had much time before someone saw them, Adam walked over to the closed door and tried the handle. To his relief, the handle moved without resistance, and Adam could feel the door start to move slightly. As quietly as he was able, he pushed the door open by a couple of inches before peeking into the room.

As his eyes adjusted to the half-light gloom inside Adam could make out a few details. A bed, shielded from view by a partly drawn ceiling height curtain running around it, was in the very centre. A large window took up much of the far wall, but any view out of the room was blocked by long blinds, currently closed, with only a few slim vertical slivers of light squeezing through where there was the odd unevenly spaced gap in the slats. One of these fell directly from the window across the bed, where Adam could make out a raised bump in the sheet, although the upper half of the bed remained hidden from sight.

Realising that he would have to enter the room to see anything further Adam turned and signaled quickly to Charlie, who was stood leaning against the far wall doing his best to look inconspicuous, alternately looking with great interest at his fingernails and turning to closely study the nearest paintings on the wall. While that meant that he now looked as suspicious as it was possible to be, as the corridor currently remained empty, it didn't seem to matter too much.

Returning to the door, Adam very slowly pushed it open further, this time making a gap sufficiently wide to squeeze through. Looking around he couldn't spot a light switch on the nearest wall, so he left the door partly open, allowing some light to continue to filter into the room. Several tentative steps took him to the edge of the heavy curtain surrounding the upper half of the bed, and drawing a deep, nervous breath Adam took the final step that took him within the curtain.

There was a small figure in the bed, hospital gown partly visible above the covers, which lay smooth and unruffled as if the occupant of the bed hadn't moved in some time. To one side of the bed there was a bank of machinery, and now he was within the curtain he could hear the regular muted beep of a monitor of some kind. Making his way around the bed Adam reached the far side and was able to see the face of its occupant for the first time. One of the slender shards of light from the window fell directly across her face, highlighting the dark bob of hair, which had grown longer and slightly uneven since Adam had last seen her.

"Nora," breathed Adam, her features recognisable even in the limited light. He looked down at her sleeping face, studying her more closely. To his mind her brow looked more furrowed than you would expect in a sleeping figure, a deep crease in the small forehead. Asleep she also looked younger, more vulnerable than he remembered her appearing when he had seen her in class.

As he stood studying her face and wondering what he was supposed to do next, he was disturbed by Charlie's shout "Twitta-woo, uh... I mean Beep!" and then the sound of running footsteps clattering off up the tiled floor of the corridor outside. This was followed a few moments later by the more measured pace of what sounded like several pairs of feet walking towards the room, accompanied by the muffled mutter of approaching voices. Adam desperately looked around the room, which held very little in the way of potential hiding places. As the door to the room swung open, he dived under the bed pulling his arms and legs in as tightly to his body as could manage.

"So there hasn't been any change?" It was a man's voice, drawing closer to the bed. Looking out from his limited viewpoint on the floor Adam presumed this voice belonged to the dark trousers and brown brogues now stood a few centimetres from his face.

"No, still nothing I am afraid," replied a second voice, female this time, which Adam identified from below the bed as belonging to a lady wearing a pair of sensible flat shoes.

"I sent her father home for a rest," she continued, "he had been with her most of the day and night for the last week and was completely exhausted bless him."

"It doesn't make any sense," said brown brogues. "Every scan, every test we have carried out has come back negative, yet she hasn't stirred or shown any reaction since she got here."

"I know," replied sensible flats, "her parents can't even tell us what happened to her, just found her like this in bed one morning and since then... nothing."

"The hospital has a specialist coming in from London next week to take a look at her," continued brown brogues pacing around the bed to stand next to the bank of monitors. "Until then all we can do is continue to keep her stable and see if anything further comes up."

"Poor little mite," said sensible flats, "to look at her you would just think she was sleeping."

Brown brogues made his way back around the bed, presumably having finished with the monitors and headed back to the doorway, pausing for a moment as he asked to be kept informed of any change in Nora's condition, then he was gone. This just left sensible flats, who fussed around the bed for a few minutes, humming softly to herself, before also leaving.

Adam waited a minute or two longer, his heart still thumping from how close he had come to being caught. Then cautiously he pulled himself out from under the bed on his hands and knees, stretching out slightly to iron out the kinks that had formed in his back while he had been hiding. Nora was lying in exactly the same position as she had been in before, her forehead still creased with worry. To Adam the impression of troubled sleep was obvious.

"Don't worry Nora," Adam muttered quietly, "I'm not quite sure how yet, but I will find a way to wake you up and get you out of your nightmare."

Adam patted down his pockets and pulled out a bag of the herbs that Grimble had given him for protection against the Nightmares. Although it was a bit of a long shot he wondered if the smell of the herbs might also help bring Nora out of her bad dream. However, as he leant out across her sleeping figure with the bag in hand, he was disturbed by a feeling of growing warmth emanating once again from the pendant around his neck. As the feeling of warmth grew the pendant slipped out from under his shirt and dangled down over Nora, the glow intensifying as it got closer to her.

While she had remained completely unmoving the entire time that Adam had been in the room up until then, for a moment he thought he saw Nora's eyelids flicker ever so slightly, the crease in her forehead relaxing by a tiny fraction. Looking from the pendant to Nora's face Adam got the definite feeling that there was some sort of connection between the two, that the proximity of the pendant might be getting some sort of reaction from her. Based on this hope, he was reaching down to move the pendant closer to Nora's face when he was disturbed by a noise across the room. Looking around to see what had caused it, almost immediately behind him stood a short, very surprised looking nurse who he presumed, after looking down for a moment, to be the owner of the sensible flat shoes from the earlier overheard discussion. Somehow, he had missed the sound of her coming back into the room and her look of surprise was rapidly changing to one of suspicion.

"I can explain," began Adam, wondering if he actually could in any way that would make sense, but was interrupted by the nurse.

"No need to explain love," she said reassuringly. "I know why you're here."

"What do you mean?" asked Adam, wondering if she had mistaken him for a member of the family.

"You are meddling," spat the nurse with a suddenly unpleasant smile, "and meddling can't be tolerated."

With that she swung up her arm with surprising speed, which turned out to be holding a heavy metal tray. Too late Adam felt the warning chill up his spine, just as he saw a momentary flash of inky blackness in the nurse's eyes. Despite this, oddly the last thought that passed through Adam's mind before he collapsed into unconsciousness was that Charlie would have been very disappointed in the nurse, who had turned out not to be very nice or cheerful at all.

CHAPTER 14

With an inward gasp of breath, Adam bolted up into a seated position, before groaning and clutching the side of his head and wincing with remembered pain. Then he realised he was back in the dream world and that the memory of pain was just that, only a memory. With that realisation the rest of his recent memories also resurfaced, and he groaned aloud again, but this time rather than a groan of pain it was one of annoyance. He had been so close to waking up Nora, he just knew it. She had definitely reacted to the pendant's warm glow, just a few more seconds and she would have been awake, and now... now he was presumably lying unconscious somewhere in the hospital room alongside the still sleeping Nora, no good to anyone. As he looked around the second thought that occurred to him was to question why he had appeared here, back in the green clearing where he had first arrived, rather than having been transported straight to Lucid and the others like the last time he had entered Reverie. For a fleeting moment before he had fully awoken, he had felt like someone's attention had been on him, but then the feeling had faded, and now he found himself back here.

He wasn't sure how much time had passed here since his last visit and couldn't help but wonder if the others had reached the Stairway by now... if they were already facing the Horror, unaware that he had failed in his attempt to wake Nora. Now he was back here in the dream world the only thing he could think to do was to try and reach them somehow, let them know that he hadn't managed to wake her and see if there was any other way he could help.

Remembering the vantage point from which Lucid had first

shown him the City of Nocturne, way off in the distance, Adam made his way across the clearing and found the same spot. The ground rose up between a break in the trees, climbing above the rest of the clearing and leading to a steep drop into the valley below, allowing a clear view across Reverie. As he stood peering out to the south, he could see the walls and clusters of housing that made up the City, and turning to the north he could just about make out the slender structure of the Stairway wavering slightly in the early morning heat. But despite its wonder, it wasn't the Stairway that held his attention, rather it was the sight of the huge and slowly twisting mass of darkness that seemed to be almost immediately upon it, something that could only be the Horror.

Adam squeezed his eyes half-closed to filter out the glare of the sun and try and see more clearly. From this distance it looked just as it had in his earlier vision. It was like one of the black whirlwinds that had appeared on the barges before, leaving patches of burning destruction in their wake, but at an infinitely bigger scale. Viewing it so far away, off on the distant horizon, Adam could lift his hand and hold his fingers to either side of the Horror, imagine squashing it between thumb and forefinger. But he knew that in reality the Horror must be impossibly huge, hundreds of meters high... and Lucid and his friends were out there, somewhere underneath its shadow.

Caught up in his worries, Adam stood completely still for a moment, the enormity of everything temporarily paralyzing him. Suddenly everything seemed too difficult, the problems just too big for him to deal with. He was just a normal boy, the sensible part of his mind told him, somehow caught up in this craziness. It wasn't his job to sort things out, he could just wait here till he got tired again, fall asleep and wake up back home. Then he could get rid of the pendant and forget that any of this had ever happened.

Trying to steady his nerves he drew a deep breath in, letting it out as slowly and calmly as he was able. Managing to tear his eyes away from the distant spinning menace of the Horror he tried to think what his friends, old and new, would advise him to do now.

He knew that Lucid would have faith that he would be able to do something, seeming to have believed that Adam was something special since their first meeting. His belief had been so strong that some of it had even rubbed off on Adam, sanding off the rough edges of his insecurities and doubts, making him think for a while that he really could be the Daydreamer that Lucid wanted him to be.

Then he thought what Charlie would say, Charlie who had risked his perfect record because of Adam's fantastical dreams, and he knew that Charlie would also believe that he was capable of doing something to help, and even if he wasn't, that he should definitely try.

Next Grimble popped into his head, Adam could almost hear his deep, grumpy voice saying, "You're an idiot and will probably get yourself killed in a really embarrassing way." Adam decided to ignore imaginary Grimble and move on.

Finally, he thought about his mother, everything she had done to prepare him for the dream world, how hard she had worked to make his ability to imagine and to dream as strong as it could be. Pushing the confusion he felt about his past and family into the background, he concentrated instead on the happy memories of time with his mum. He thought about how much he missed her, and the knowledge that she was here, somewhere in the dream world waiting for him, and as he did he could finally feel his indecision fading.

Muttering to himself that it was a terrible idea and that imaginary Grimble was almost certainly going to be right on this one, he closed his eyes and took a tentative step closer to the drop into the valley. Keeping his eyes squeezed closed he started to try and clear his mind and think back to the memories he had used in the gardens with Lucid when he had first tried out his daydreaming. As he did so he took another small step forward, then another, fairly sure that by now he should either be at, or slightly beyond, the edge of the small plateau. It was surprisingly hard to keep his mind clear when all he could now imagine was what it would be like to land with a splat on the ground below. But he tried all the same, taking one final step forward and then opening his eyes.

Not particularly wanting to look down, he did so anyway and immediately felt sick. He was indeed no longer on the ground, but instead of being a few metres off the ground he was floating many times that over the floor of the valley, the tops of the trees that lined it quite some distance below him and looking decidedly pointy from this angle.

This time, rather than letting panic overwhelm him, Adam managed to control his emotions, lifting his gaze from the valley floor and concentrating on the sight of the Stairway off in the distance. Willing himself forward he could feel the wind brushing against his cheeks as he started to move, the building pressure flattening his hair against the top of his head as he picked up speed. Despite himself Adam began to grin, and fairly safe in the knowledge that no one could see him, he tried out a couple of superhero poses, one arm outstretched in front of him. His smile widened as he picked up more and more speed... and then vanished completely as he suddenly crashed straight through the middle of a flock of unusually coloured and extremely surprised birds.

A few seconds later he was clear of the other side of the flock, back in the open sky and somehow still in control. This time however he didn't allow himself any celebration, just concentrated on his destination and on moving as fast as he could manage. The journey that had taken more than a day on the Dreamskipper passed in a matter of minutes, the distance rapidly swallowed up as the ground and the swell of the Weave passed far below him.

While only a passing distraction, Adam was incredibly relieved to spot a cluster of Barges making their slow way along one of the winding avenues of the Weave as he drew closer to his destination. Although fewer in number than he remembered, they were undeniably the same as those of the Assembly, the larger Grand Barge in the centre of the little convoy particularly recognisable.

A few minutes later and Adam was drawing close to the Stairway. The nearer he got the more obvious the incredible scale of both the Stairway and the approaching Horror became. Even at the height he was approaching, both towered above him. The broad top of the whirling Horror was a good hundred metres above him and the Stairway continued upwards into the sky further than Adam was able to see. The closer he got the more he also struggled to maintain the smoothness of his flight. Even though it was still some distance away the violence of the approaching Horror was disrupting the air around him, making it increasingly hard to control his movements. Realising that it was going to be too dangerous to continue Adam angled himself towards the ground, trying to spot where Lucid and the others might be. Just as he was about to give up on finding them, he spotted a small cluster of figures about halfway between the Stairway and the approaching Horror, the figures looking incredibly tiny in comparison to their surroundings.

As he approached Adam was caught by a particularly violent gust of wind, knocking him to one side and turning the last few metres of his descent into an out of control spinning mess before he hit the ground. He bounced a couple of times, barreling past a shocked looking Lucid. He then rolled between an equally stunned Henry and the Lady, somehow avoiding hitting either, before finally sliding directly into an even more surprised Grimble, bringing him to a sudden halt in a tangle of arms and legs.

Disentangling himself slowly and painfully Adam looked up at the surprised and concerned, and in one case muddy and angry, faces that were gathering above him.

"You should have seen the rest of my flight," he managed to murmur, "it was amazing."

"Idiot," he heard Grimble growl behind him as he slowly got to his feet, "what in the great dream are you doing here?"

"Trying to get to you," Adam replied, a little defensively. The fact that he had managed to fly all the way to them not getting the recognition he felt it deserved. Not really knowing where to start with an explanation, he jumped straight to what seemed the most important.

"I... I wasn't able to save Nora," he began, seeing Lucid's shoulders slump as he said it. "I'm sorry, I really tried... and she is definitely involved in this. There was a Nightmare with her, and it stopped me before I was able to wake her up."

"Then we have lost," he heard Henry say just off to one side. "The Horror is just too big. We have also failed in our attempts to stop it. It is only a matter of minutes now until it reaches the Stairway and then..." he tailed off, the look of misery on his face telling the rest of the story clearly enough.

"Isn't there anything else?" asked Adam desperately, not wanting to believe that he could have made it all the way here just to sit and watch helplessly.

"I don't believe so," replied Lucid sympathetically, helping Adam to his feet as he continued. "I am sure you did everything you could do Adam, as have we all."

Grimble cast a venomous look up at the Horror as he spoke. "We tried to channel some of the Weave towards it, to push it back or block its movement, but it seems impossible to balance out so much darkness." He was holding one of his arms gingerly with the other, a dark stain burned across the sleeve of his robe and a matching, raw-looking mark on the skin of his hand. "Every time we tried, we were forced to retreat, the last time only just getting away in one piece."

Despite having only just managed to get back to his feet after his collision with Adam, he dropped back down into a sitting position, the constant anger that powered him seeming to drain away, making him look smaller and older than normal.

Adam could understand Grimble's despair. Although it was still several minutes away from reaching them, even at this distance he could feel the sheer venom and power of the approaching Horror. The disturbed wind buffeted at his face, feeling unnaturally sharp on his skin, while the sky above him seemed incredibly bleak, the darkness of the towering whirl-wind blocking out the sun. The combination of the wind and the loss of the warm sunlight also meant that Adam was feeling increasingly cold, as if the chilling sensation up and down his spine that had warned him in the past of approaching Nightmares had spread across his whole body.

However, while the cold was beginning to affect his body, stiffening his muscles and slowing his movement, it was having the opposite effect on his mind, which was racing. Adam refused to believe that after everything they had been through, that there was nothing more they could do now. Then a thought, previously nestled at the back of his mind, pushed its way forward shouting for his attention. He remembered the view as he had flown in towards the Stairway, the sight of the land laid out below him and the strands of the Weave running across the landscape.

"Lucid," he said urgently, "do you still have the map you used earlier?"

"Yes," Lucid confirmed, sounding confused "but why would you want it?"

"Can you just show me?" asked Adam. "Please, it's important."

Lucid walked across to where the group had piled equipment and a few supplies and returned with the map, unrolling it before placing it on an upturned crate used as a makeshift table. Adam's brain felt like it was fizzing inside his skull as he tried to put his thoughts in order. The map seemed to confirm the bizarre thought that had come to him as he had viewed the Weave from above.

"You remember before you said about going to the Library, not your Library but the one back in my world?" asked Adam.

"Yes I do, but..." began Lucid, but Adam cut him off in his sudden enthusiasm, his words almost tripping over each other in their keenness to be heard.

"I found something in one of the books I read. I was going to ask you about it, but I forgot until now. I found a picture of something called a Dreamcatcher, the book said it was an old Native American method of protecting children from bad dreams."

This drew blank looks from the others, but although the description didn't seem to register with them, Adam pressed on, increasingly convinced that he was on to something.

"I started to wonder if that idea had come from here too, that someone had seen something in a dream, maybe even another Daydreamer like me, and they had taken the idea back home with them."

He paused for a moment patting his pockets, "Do you have a pen and paper?"

Lucid shook his head, but Henry stepped forward and offered a scrap of paper and an old fountain pen to him.

The companions were all leaning in now, caught up in Adam's excitement despite themselves. "It came to me when I remembered the view of the Weave from above, and now looking at the map...." said Adam sketching out a rough illustration of a Dreamcatcher on the paper and laying it down alongside the map.

"Do you see it?" he asked, "If you look at them side by side, the Weave looks like a giant dreamcatcher, it's just the threads are the channels of the Weave as it flows around Reverie... and it's centred on the Stairway, on where we are right now!"

He looked around at the others, breathing heavily as he finished his explanation, desperate for some sort of confirmation that he was right, that it wasn't just another crazy thought.

"It's a strange coincidence to be sure," said Henry uncertainly, "although I don't remember ever reading anything about such things."

"Still," broke in Grimble gruffly, "we don't exactly have many options left." He stopped and looked up at the approaching Horror "...or much time" he added. "So for once I suppose we could see if there is more in the boy's head than fluff."

Lucid looked across at Adam enquiringly. "What do you propose?"

"I'm not completely sure," replied Adam, moving closer to the nearest shore of the Weave, "there is something I would like to try though."

As he reached the edge, he could almost feel the dreams of the Weave calling to him, telling him deep in his bones what he had to do next. He knelt on the grassy bank and without pausing for long enough to let any serious doubts develop, he thrust both his hands deep into the rolling mist.

He wasn't sure what he was expecting, but all that he felt was a gentle tickle on his forearms. Adam closed his eyes concentrating completely on the feeling of the Weave flowing around him, letting his mind free to do the rest. He pictured the red of the Dreamcatcher's crisscross threads and then the view of the Weave as he had seen it from above, slowly blurring them into one image in his mind. As he concentrated, he could feel the familiar warmth of the pendant on his chest, increasingly hot as he held the thought steady in his mind. At the very edge of his perception he heard a gasp of amazement that sounded like Lucid, although it seemed to have come from somewhere far, far away.

The heat of the pendant was becoming painful but in his mind the job wasn't completely finished, so gritting his teeth Adam continued to imagine the Weave forming one enormous Dreamcatcher, big enough to protect a whole world from bad dreams. Just as the burning sensation from the pendant became almost unbearable, he felt a hand on his shoulder and a voice broke through his concentration. "Adam, Adam... look."

Opening his eyes the first things he saw were his hands, still thrust into the Weave but with the surrounding mist now coloured a light red, as it had been in his mind. Almost not daring to look any further, he slowly raised his gaze and looking out he could see the strands of the Weave heading off into the distance, each one now a mass of glowing crimson, exactly as he had imagined.

Realising that the others weren't all sharing his view, he turned to see what else could possibly have drawn their attention. As soon as he did it was obvious what they were all looking at, the Horror was changing in front of their eyes. The previous direct line it had taken toward the Stairway was wavering, the Horror twisting queasily from side to side without its previous sense of purpose and direction. At its edges the shadowy whirl-wind was starting to lose its definition, sections of it tearing away as it twisted, and then fizzling into nothingness as they left the main body. Despite its incredible scale and ferocity, the Horror seemed completely trapped by the surrounding glow of the Weave and was rapidly shrinking.

While the others simply stood in rapt attention, Grimble was the most animated that Adam had ever seen him, bouncing up and down on the balls of his feet, punching his hands towards the weakening Horror and shouting a selection of very colour-ful insults.

Within minutes the Horror had shrunk to a fraction of its former size and while it still loomed over the companions, it was without the same sense of threat and menace, now insig-nificant compared to the towering Stairway.

"We've done it," said Lucid, his face a picture of delighted surprise.

"No," added Grimble from behind Adam, squeezing his shoul-der in congratulations "Not we… you… you have done it Adam. Much as it amazes me to say it, it seems that you really are a Day-dreamer… a proper one."

Then seeming to remember himself he coughed awkwardly, adding, "Don't let it go to your head though, I am sure that beginner's luck also has a lot to do with it."

But as he spoke Adam saw the Lady lift her hand in warning and point back at the Horror. Its erratic movement had now completely ceased, and it now stood slowly spinning on the spot. As they stared the base of the Horror rippled lazily for a moment, the shredded darkness parted, and a figure stepped out from within it.

CHAPTER 15

The new arrival moved further from the base of the Horror, walking slowly towards them, the dark strands that clung to its arms and legs falling away as it approached, shed like old skin from a snake. As it drew closer Adam could see that it was a man, tall and strongly built, with long, unkempt blonde hair. He felt Grimble's hands, previously squeezing his shoulders in congratulation, suddenly tense. His short, strong fingers were now digging into his back far more painfully. At the same time he heard Grimble make a low choking sound deep in his throat, and then say disbelievingly "Isenbard?"

The man had now almost reached them, his long confident stride closing the distance between them quickly. As he approached Adam could see his face more clearly, the intelligent blue eyes and friendly smile recognisable from the painting in the portrait corridor.

"Greetings old friend," said Isenbard, his voice strong and clear, looking over Adam's shoulder directly at Grimble. "Who would have thought we would meet again in such a place."

Grimble released his grip on Adam's shoulders and stepped around in front of him. The gruffness that Adam was used to hearing was almost entirely gone from his voice when he answered, instead he sounded desperately sad and slightly lost.

"Isenbard, how... I saw you fall into a Horror, I thought you were gone, I thought you were..."

Isenbard gave a low chuckle, the sound of which was far less pleasant than the cheerful grin that remained on his handsome face.

"Oh Grimble," he gently chastised, "always so literal, so sens-

146

ible." He gestured towards the Horror, "I did fall into a Horror and it was..." he paused, a cold look passing across his friendly expression for a moment, like a bank of cloud passing briefly in front of the sun "...an interesting experience."

"But," he continued, "I survived... with some help. You would be amazed what you can learn if you are willing to open your mind."

"But why didn't you come back?" Grimble asked, his voice still plaintive. "Why this?" he added, pointing to the Horror.

Isenbard smiled more broadly at the question. "As I said, it's amazing what you can learn, and one of the things that I learned is that the other world, the Waking World, is much closer than we were led to believe, much more..." he paused for a moment while looking for the right word "...accessible. I found that it was possible to go there for a short time and there is so much, so very much there that I want. So many minds, so many possibilities if you only think big enough."

"But this doesn't help you," Lucid cut in, a tremor in his voice as he spoke. "None of this helps you, to attack the Stairway would just do terrible damage to our world."

"Wrong!" shouted Isenbard, in a deep growling voice, far removed from the friendly expression that remained on his face, his voice instantly returning to its normal pleasant tone as he continued.

"Very, very wrong. Without the Stairway I have it on very good authority..." he shuddered again for a moment as he spoke "...very good authority indeed, that the barriers between the worlds would be removed, giving me as much access to the Waking World as I want... and as it turns out I want that a lot."

He moved his mocking gaze away from Grimble for a moment. "And I am not the only one who wants that, am I my dear."

Adam turned his head to see who Isenbard was talking to and found himself looking at the downturned eyes of the Lady, who seemed unable to meet Isenbard's gaze.

"You?" said Lucid unbelievingly, "was it you that betrayed us?" His voice became stronger and increasingly angry as he continued, "you that put my people in danger?"

Still seemingly unable to look up the Lady replied quietly, her oddly layered voice sounding younger and more uncertain than Adam was used to.

"I'm sorry, truly I am... I didn't know what he was going to do..." her voice trailed off for a moment, then she took a deep breath in and continued. "I just wanted..." she paused, swallowing heavily, and tried again. "I can feel the Weave calling me back, my time in the world is coming to an end and I wanted... I wanted to stay."

She raised her eyes to stare across at Isenbard, accusations obvious in her gaze. "You told me that if the barrier between the worlds fell then I would be free, that I would be able to stay."

Isenbard returned her look with a wolfish grin on his face, "and what do you think now?" he said, his tone mocking.

The Lady looked directly at him for a moment, the blue in her eyes flashing dangerously before the strength went out of them and she looked down once again. "Now I think that you lied," she replied softly.

"Quite right," said Isenbard the smile remaining on his face, "but you have been a great help none the less."

Isenbard turned back to look at Adam, his expression changing to one of curiosity. "Which brings me to you, little Daydreamer."

He pointed to the diminished Horror and sighed theatrically "Look at what you have done to my beautiful nightmare."

Adam looked back defiantly "Yes, so what? We have beaten it... and beaten you."

"You would think so, wouldn't you," said Isenbard, still smiling, "and it took me so much effort. I had to find a really strong dreamer to make such a Horror, I searched for years to find just the right one, a young impressionable mind, but strong, so very strong, and then..." his eyes narrowed "...then after I find her, it turns out that a Daydreamer, your interfering mother, was close by and threatened to ruin all of my careful work."

He gave a pleasant, cheerful laugh, as if remembering a well-loved joke they all shared, and shrugged his shoulders, "honestly, what were the chances of that?"

For a moment the friendly façade faded again and Isenbard's handsome features became ugly as his face filled with remembered anger.

"Even then your Mother somehow escaped me," he snarled, almost spitting the words at Adam.

Then, just as quickly as it had appeared on his face, the anger passed and he continued in a pleasant and friendly voice once again, as if nothing had happened. "Which brings me to you Adam, another Daydreamer it seems. Not anywhere near as talented as you Mother but somehow..." he pointed at the glowing Weave, "somehow able to do all of this. I can't help but wonder if you had some help, perhaps something left to you by your Mother. Something I would dearly like."

Without thinking, Adam moved a hand to protectively cover the spot where the pendant hung under his t-shirt, a reaction that was not lost on Isenbard.

"As I thought," said Isenbard, with a hungry look towards the place where the pendant still hung. "That saves me the trouble of any further searching. It almost makes all the difficulty you have caused me worthwhile."

As he spoke Grimble and Lucid walked around Adam and stood between him and Isenbard.

"You have lost," said Grimble, a little of the previous strength returning to his voice "and you are in no position to make any more threats."

Henry also took his place next to them, although a little more hesitantly.

"Yes... you... you should leave Adam alone, you... you... are an extremely unpleasant man," he said, with a slight stammer.

Isenbard simply smiled even more broadly and raised his hands, palms outstretched. "So brave aren't you, so brave stood alongside your friends, scared little man." He looked around as if noticing something for the first time, "and here I am, all alone, whatever can I do."

He lifted his hands higher as he continued, for a minute making it look like he was raising them in surrender. "As I said before, it is amazing what you can learn if you have an open mind. Let me show you something else I have learned."

As he finished speaking black strands shot from his open hands, arcing high over the companion's heads. Adam's eyes followed the course of their flight and he saw them plummet into the ground, perhaps a hundred metres away. Where each one landed there was a slight shimmer in the air and then a shadowy figure formed in its place. Adam stared in disbelief as he saw the shadow begin to solidify and within moments he was looking at a fully formed Nightmare, this one in the shape of a large snake, twisting and coiling on the spot... and looking extremely angry.

Looking from left to right he could see a dozen more Nightmares appearing, blinking into existence wherever the darkness Isenbard had released had landed.

As Isenbard concentrated on his summoning of the Nightmares, Grimble looked across at Lucid and Adam.

"Listen, there is still a chance you can get to Nora," he hissed. "You might have failed to wake her in your world, but her dreaming self is right there, in the middle of the Horror." He reached inside his robes and pulled out one of his bags of herbs, hefting it in his hands. "We're not done yet. Try and find her, we will buy you as much time as we can."

Lucid gulped as he looked at the massing numbers of the shadowy Nightmares, adding, "Which may not be all that long."

He reached down and picked up one of the long poles he had used to punt the Dreamskipper and looked across at the Nightmares, obviously mentally weighing one against the other and finding the pole rather lacking as a means of defence. Then he appeared to have a moment of inspiration. He cautiously dipped the ends of the pole into the red glow of the Weave, which slowly wrapped itself around it, strands of mist hanging from either end.

"Interesting," he said, adding, "this might at least give the Nightmares a headache for a while," and managed a weak smile.

Henry also stepped forward, although he didn't say anything, just nodded at Adam before turning away to face the horde of monsters that were forming up behind them.

Isenbard had finished his summoning and looked with satisfaction at the mass of Nightmares that now stood, slithered or crawled close to Adam and his companions. He then turned his gaze back to Grimble and the others and a sneer once again marred his face.

"Do you really think you can do anything to them, anything to me? You have achieved nothing. My Nightmares will take you all and I will rebuild the Horror without your interference."

He paused for a moment, his expression changing from one of anger to rapture. "The Stairway will fall, and I will have all the access I want to both of your worlds." He closed his eyes, appearing to savor the thought. "Can you imagine the terrible dreams that I will bring."

"No," broke in a voice, quietly but clearly, "you will not." The Lady stepped forward, her blue eyes blazing. "I am ashamed, I was afraid to return to the Weave, afraid to give up the life that I had become used to... and you used that against me, made me something less than I should be."

She looked across for a moment, letting her gaze settle briefly upon each of the other companions. "But I am less afraid of that than the world you intend to bring. If I am to return to the Weave I will go in a manner of my choosing."

As she spoke this final word, she ran directly at Isenbard, her feet moving over the uneven ground at an incredible pace. He had begun to lift his hands in defence as she approached, but she was so impossibly fast that they were only raised halfway by the time she reached him, by this point a glowing blur. She lowered her shoulders and wrapped her arms around him tightly as they crashed together. Her momentum was sufficient to drive them both back into the mass of the Horror and they vanished within the whirling darkness.

For what felt like an incredibly long, stretched-out moment in time they all stood transfixed, concentrating on the sudden and unexpected clash that had just taken place, staring at the spot where Isenbard and the Lady had vanished. Then the temporary tranquility was broken by a very noisy and unpleasant mix of roars, hisses and other less recognisable noises from the mass of Nightmares gathered behind them. Rather than disappearing along with Isenbard, they seemed infuriated and Adam could see them beginning to advance.

Torn by indecision, Adam found himself unable to move, incapable of deciding what to do. To one side were his three remaining companions standing in the way of what could only be described as an army of Nightmares, to the other was the Horror, the concentrated mass of darkness now lit by a small but still fiercely burning spark of light somewhere deep within it.

His mind was made up by Lucid who shook him rather roughly by the shoulder and then pointed across to the Horror. "Now is our chance Adam, go to Nora and release her from her dream. If you can get to her then all of this, the Horror, the Nightmares, everything will be over."

The approaching Nightmares were now only a score of metres away "...and quickly if you don't mind," snapped Grimble, throwing the first of his burning bags of herbs into the Nightmares, several of them fading back into formless smoke as the bag burst amongst them.

Lucid turned back to face the monsters, flexing his long fingers one at a time and much to Adam's surprise, also humming quietly to himself. Although it was hardly the time, Adam realised that it sounded very like the same tune that they had all danced together to on the Grand Barge. Just behind Grimble, visibly shaking with nerves, stood Henry. He looked completely out of place, lost away from the City and the quiet peace and safety of the library, definitely not designed for the kind of challenge they now faced. Despite all of this he stood side by side with the others, which to Adam made it about the bravest thing he had ever seen.

All of these thoughts went through Adam's mind in the matter of a few seconds, and despite the fact that he desperately wanted to stay and help his friends, he knew deep down that Lucid was right. There was no other way to stop everything that was happening without finding and waking Nora. So, although it felt entirely wrong to leave them, Adam turned and ran as fast as he was able away from his friends and towards the Horror, taking one final look over his shoulder before he reached it.

The last view he had was of Lucid, Grimble and Henry with the tumultuous mass of Nightmares nearly upon them, three small, brave points of defiant light facing a tidal wave of darkness, and then he hit the edge of the Horror and the outside world faded away.

He expected to feel some sort of resistance or worse, but instead passed through the outer skin of the Horror easily, even smoothly. It was almost the same sensation as diving under the surface of the water at his local swimming pool and with it came the same sense of sudden unreality, the same feeling that you are immediately in a different world even though the surface might only be centimetres away. As he did everything went quiet. The roar of the Nightmares, the rush of the wind, all of the sounds of the outside world completely disappeared, leaving only an eerie silence.

He turned and put his hand against the outer shell he had just broken through, which had reformed and now felt solid, although slightly tacky and unpleasant, to touch. If he concentrated Adam could occasionally still also get a brief glimpse of the outside world, but these were infrequent and disjointed, wavering snapshots rather than anything more. Turning back to face the interior of the Horror, he took in his new surroundings.

The inside of the Horror was both smaller and more normal-looking than he might have imagined. It felt like being in a large cave, but with the walls, floors, and ceiling formed of the same dark shadowy substance. If you stared closely everything was also very slowly moving, less permanent and solid than it might first appear to be. Looking for a moment up above his head Adam could see that there were still flashes of light coming from somewhere within the Horror, but it was impossible to make out exactly where they might be coming from. Despite all of this, the majority of his attention was taken up by the sight of a small, forlorn figure stood right in the centre of everything.

It was undoubtedly Nora, she was dressed exactly the same as when Adam had last seen her, in a long dark blue hospital gown. While her eyes were open, she didn't seem to notice that Adam was there. In fact, as he drew closer it seemed she couldn't see anything around her at all, but rather was concentrating on some unseen vision that took all of her attention. She looked exhausted and was swaying slightly as she stood, her hair bedraggled and skin looking pale and drawn.

Pushing any other distractions to one side, Adam walked quickly over towards her, determined that this time he would not fail and knowing that he had no time to waste. Remembering the effect it had on her the last time he had seen her, he pulled the pendant from under his t-shirt as he approached and held it tightly in his right hand, hoping that it would react as it had before. But as he was about to reach her, he was disturbed by a sound from almost directly behind him, a soft but unmistakable shift in the otherwise still air.

"Stop!" said a commanding voice. Despite his determination Adam found himself slowing, his legs no longer fully under his control, and he turned to see who had spoken.

Behind him stood Isenbard, looking drained but undefeated. Despite his apparent tiredness, his face still held its self-assured smile, his eyes still twinkled with amusement at jokes to which only he knew the punchlines.

"You really don't give up do you?" he asked. "So much work, so much time and you and your group of misfits think that you can stop me, stop everything that I have spent so long building."

He took a single step towards Adam and as he did the entire Horror seemed to waver and pulse in time with his footstep. "You think you are so clever with your little dreaming tricks don't you boy, but this is my domain," he said. "In here it is my dreams that decide how the world works, not yours."

He took another step closer, the Horror again pulsing as his foot made contact with the ground, more violently this time, nearly making Adam fall.

"I will take that," he said, pointing to the pendant. "I will find your precious, trouble-making mother and the only disappointment I have is that you won't be around to see it."

He took a further step and the ground shook again in time. Now unable to keep his footing, Adam dropped to his knees as the world tremored around him. By this point Isenbard had nearly reached him, and despite his fear, Adam looked up to face him defiantly. It was then, for the briefest fraction of a second he saw something in Isenbard's face that surprised him. Only for a moment, but long enough to be pretty sure, Adam saw a flicker of fear pass across the clear blue eyes. A tiny crack in the façade of confidence and disdain.

But why, he thought to himself, why would Isenbard be afraid? It was very clear that here, inside the Horror, he was no match for him. He could hardly even stand and yet... his mother's letter flashed through his brain once more and the last words again came to the forefront of his mind, "You must save Nora," and he realised why Isenbard was afraid. Everything that Isenbard was doing was to draw Adam's attention, to keep it focused away from Nora, to keep Adam from doing what he had come here for in the first place. Adam mentally kicked himself and concentrated on getting moving again, overcoming the paralysis that Isenbard was trying to force on him.

Although it was incredibly difficult Adam slowly pushed himself back into a standing position, still focusing on Isenbard for the moment, keeping the pendant clutched protectively in his closed fist. Isenbard was now only a few steps away, with a triumphant look upon his face, and as he approached Adam tensed himself. But rather than trying to face Isenbard, at the last moment he turned and instead pushed himself as hard as he could manage away from him and towards Nora, putting all of his strength into one impossibly long leaping dive across the room.

He heard Isenbard shout in fury behind him as he leapt, but he didn't look back, his attention now fully on Nora. Time seemed to slow as he flew through the air towards her, the atmosphere thickening as if the air itself within the Horror was trying to hold him back. He felt an unpleasant sensation tugging at his ankle and to either side he could see further tendrils of smoky darkness winding their way through the air towards him. Clutching the pendant tightly he concentrated as hard as he was able, trying to block out all of the surrounding distractions and felt a familiar warmth begin to flow around him. His movement through the air eased slightly and he could feel the grasp of the darkness on his ankle loosen as the warming glow spread throughout his body.

After what seemed like an eternity, but in reality must have been only a few fractions of a second, Adam reached Nora, the fingertips of his free hand reaching out and clutching her shoulder. He pulled himself in closer to her, the pendant's glow becoming almost unbearably bright, surrounding both Adam and Nora in a welcoming cocoon of light.

Everything faded around him for a moment and when his vision blinked back he found himself alone with Nora in a direct replica of her hospital room but formed again from the shadowy substance that made up the Horror. She was sitting up in the bed, clutching her arms around her knees and staring at him.

"Who are you?" she asked him hesitantly.

"I'm Adam," he replied, walking slowly towards her, "I'm here to help you."

"I don't like it here," Nora said, pulling her knees more tightly in towards her body, not seeming to have really heard him. "I've been on my own and it's dark… I don't like the dark, it gives me nightmares."

"Don't worry," Adam told her as confidently as he could. "I'm going to make sure you get home, back to your family and away from here."

This time his words seemed to get through to her and Nora's eyes widened in hope.

"I'd like that," she said, "I'd like to go home."

Tentatively Adam held out the pendant towards her one last time and gently taking her hand placed it along with his tightly around it. The previous glow immediately returned and intensified, and with a sudden disorientating flash Adam found himself back in the Horror once again, holding on to Nora and with the glow of the pendant still surrounding them both.

He could hear Isenbard raging behind him, but the sound seemed increasingly distant and to either side he could see the darkness of the Horror start to rip itself apart, sections tearing away and fluttering harmlessly into the sky, revealing glimpses of the outside world.

After a few moments the glow became so bright that Adam couldn't see anything outside of the light that surrounded him, having to squeeze his eyes tightly closed as it became too painful to see. Then everything faded into the background and darkness came again, but this time it was a warm and comfortable blackness that felt like sleep, felt like safety and home.

CHAPTER 16

Adam's eyelids fluttered, a gentle light leaking through and causing small spots of colour to dance in his vision for a moment before his eyes fully opened. His head ached terribly and as he looked slowly around, he realised that he was still lying on the floor in Nora's hospital room. The tiled floor was cold against his back and his muscles felt stiff as he tried to raise himself into a seated position.

As he pushed down on the floor, he could feel the pressure of the pendant still clasped tightly in his hand, although it now felt cold and lifeless, all sensations of the earlier warming glow gone. He carefully stowed it back under his t-shirt and despite the awkward painfulness of his movements pushed himself up off the ground. Trying his best to ignore the temporary nausea that flooded through him, he managed to get to his feet and there, directly in front of him, was Nora's hospital bed.

Feeling almost unbearably nervous, Adam approached her, his heart pounding, full of desperate unexpressed hope, and as he reached the side of the bed, he risked a look down at Nora's face. Adam couldn't initially see any change, but then he noticed that the furrow in her forehead seemed to be relaxing, her sleeping face looked less troubled than before. To one side of the bed he heard the steady beep of the monitor fluctuate for a moment and then a low, persistent alarm began to sound. As it did Adam saw Nora turn her head slightly to one side, in reaction to the noise.

Realising that the alarm was likely to draw attention to the room sooner rather than later and knowing that he had no reasonable explanation for being there, Adam regretfully muttered a quick goodbye to Nora, and with a final look back over his shoulder, headed out of the small room. It was with a strange sense of unreality that he made his way back up the yellow corridor, the bright walls and children's pictures so far removed from the Horror he had just left behind. Slowly the realisation that he had returned safely home sunk in, and more than that, that he had managed somehow to get through to Nora. A slight smile began to form at the edge of his mouth and his stride became more buoyant as he continued down the corridor.

"Adam!" a worried voice broke into his thoughts and brought him back to the present. Charlie walked hurriedly over to him as he entered the main reception area.

"Adam, there you are, I thought maybe you had been caught in Nora's room... sorry that I ran away, I got a really funny look when I did the owl noise and I panicked."

Adam grinned broadly at his friend, feeling for the first time that he was truly back home.

"We did it," he told Charlie, "I think that Nora is going to be okay."

"What happened?" asked Charlie, wide-eyed. "Tell me everything... and I mean absolutely everything!"

"It might take a while to explain," Adam replied. "Let's find a spot where we can talk."

And so they did, finding a quiet corner of the reception area, far from the desk and the main doors. For the next hour Adam tried his best to summarise everything that had happened, although he still brushed over some of the more terrifying moments, which he was as keen as possible to forget. Just as he was finishing his story, he spotted a tired and worried looking middle-aged couple enter the reception, deep in excited, animated conversation. Pausing briefly to talk to the receptionist they were almost immediately met by a doctor who escorted them down the corridor that led to the children's ward.

"Come on," said Adam, "I want to see this... just to be sure."

Charlie nodded keenly, understanding and sharing Adam's enthusiasm. Staying far back enough to not be seen Adam and

Charlie followed the couple back through the hospital corridors, treading the familiar route back down the yellow corridor and to the small room at the far end. The door to Nora's room was closed by the time Adam and Charlie reached it and Adam knew that they had no reason or excuse for going in, but the sound of the relieved voices and happy tears he could hear through the door was reward enough.

* * *

Two weeks passed, most of which was spent either in school or in detention. The remainder of the time in between was spent permanently grounded at Charlie's house. Unable to tell the real story of where they had gone, or why, Adam and Charlie had accepted these punishments without complaint, both entirely sure that it had been well worth it.

Then, at the start of the third week and without any great fanfare, Nora returned to their class. Miss Grudge simply reintroduced her, saying that she was now returning to school as normal. When Charlie had offered once again for her to sit next to him, although this time just for the one day, Adam had moved without complaint.

Containing his excitement at seeing her fully recovered and returned to school he sat at the back of the class lost in his thoughts, memories of the last time he had seen her still fresh in his mind. Then rather slowly, even hesitantly, Adam saw her turn in her seat and look back across her shoulder at him. Half covered by her now more neatly trimmed fringe, her eyes met his, containing a look of quizzical recognition. She smiled shyly and then quickly looked down and away from him. While she didn't look back again for the rest of the class, Adam couldn't shake the feeling that there were definitely going to be some awkward conversations to come.

* * *

That evening he chatted with Charlie in the spare room, talking once again, as they had every night, about the events of the last few weeks. By now Charlie had been filled in on most of the details of Adam's time in Reverie, had become familiar with Lucid, Grimble and the others that Adam had met, to the point where he felt he knew them himself. He knew about the Horror, the Weave and the travelling Sornette, the City of Nocturne and the Stairway, but the big questions remained unanswered and these were the ones they came back to every evening.

"I'm sorry there is still no news on your mum," said Charlie. "After everything you have been through it doesn't seem fair that you haven't found her."

Adam pondered this for a moment, turning the pendant over and over in his hand as he did so. It had remained entirely cold and lifeless ever since he had returned from Reverie with Nora, but he kept it with him all the time, spending its days hanging around his neck and its nights snuggly under his pillow, clasped in his hand.

Despite everything that he had been through the pendant remained a complete mystery to him, but he was absolutely sure that there was far more to discover. He was also pretty sure this was the reason why he hadn't returned to Reverie since the clash with Isenbard, his nights having been surprisingly restful but empty of dreams. He knew he should be relieved to be back home safely with Charlie, be happy that Nora was safe and well and that life had returned to some sort of normality, but deep down he desperately missed the dream world and the odd characters he had met. He was also equally desperate to know what had become of them after he had left, with the last sight he had of them being so close to being overwhelmed by the Nightmares.

Even more painful than that was the knowledge that somewhere in the dream world his mother was there, waiting for him and that she could still be in danger. While he had destroyed the Horror, he had an uncomfortable feeling that it wasn't the last he would ever see of Isenbard... and that something else, something even worse was out there pulling Isenbard's strings.

Snapping out of his thoughts he answered Charlie's implied question. "I will find my Mum," he said, as confidently as he could, trying to convince himself as much as Charlie. "She is there, somewhere in Reverie, I just need to get back there somehow."

"I know she is... and I am sure you will find her," said Charlie sympathetically. Adam nodded but didn't say anything else, not really wanting to prolong the discussion about his mother any further. Despite this, his thoughts went back once again to the message he had received from his mum on the Weave, and Grimble's promise that they would find her together.

"I'm going to turn in if you don't mind," he said, "I'm feeling pretty tired".

"Sure," said Charlie, "I'll see you in the morning then. Goodnight mate."

* * *

As he stood cleaning his teeth in the family bathroom Adam looked at himself in the mirror, trying to see if he looked any older, more heroic. If he looked like someone that had saved a world, but he didn't really seem to look any different to before. Same scruffy hair, same distracted look, same slightly uneven ears, but nothing special that he could see. Sighing to himself, he leant back to gargle some mouthwash, but when he leant forward to spit it out into the sink, he was so surprised by the sight in the mirror that he ended up dribbling it down his chin instead.

Under his t-shirt he could see a very gentle, but still visible, glow shining through the material, centred on his mum's pendant. The glow was so slight that he couldn't feel any of the previously familiar heat, but it was definitely glowing.

He ran back to his bed, nearly tripping over in his haste to get there, diving under the covers and banging his head down on to the pillow, closing his eyes tightly and thinking "sleep, sleep, sleep," as he did so. All of which was of course completely pointless as he now felt as wide awake as he had at any point in the last couple of weeks. Rather than sleeping he wanted to jump wildly around the room, punching the air and shouting happily. Because of this, it was well past midnight and late into the following morning when long overdue tiredness finally took the place of the new excitement fizzing around in Adam's brain and he managed to fall asleep.

CHAPTER 17

Adam opened his eyes, squinting into the morning light and feeling the warmth of the sun on his face. As the blurry mist of sleep was blinked clear of his pupils he was greeted by the familiar sight of a wide friendly face grinning broadly down at him.

"You decided to come back then..."

-THE END-

A SHORT WORD
FROM THE AUTHOR

I hope you have enjoyed the world of Reverie and Adam's first adventures. If you did it would be great if you could take two minutes to leave a quick review.

If you want to keep up with the latest events in Reverie you can follow the 'Daydreamer Chronicles' on Facebook. There is also the occasional update on the series website: www.daydreamerchronicles.com

Adam's adventures in Reverie continue in the second book in the Daydreamer Chronicles: Welcome to Moonshine. Read on for a taster of the next book.

WELCOME TO MOONSHINE: PROLOGUE

'Flapjack' Johnson was running. He was finding the experience less than enjoyable, it having been a very long time since he had last tried it. The bulkiness of his body, which most of the time he found to be useful, and which other people generally found intimidating, was definitely working against him now. Already he could feel a sharp pain in his side, the early start of a stitch that he knew was only going to get worse, but the discomfort didn't stop him, if anything it spurred him to go even faster. He was pretty certain that the pain he was experiencing as a result of running was a lot less than that he could expect if he dared stop.

"Typical," he thought to himself bitterly as he skidded around a corner, heavy flat feet struggling to gain traction on the damp floor. Moonshine had been a new start for him, the place was weird, true enough, but as a result the other residents didn't seem that fussy about who lived there. For him that had been enough. He wasn't entirely sure where, or even why, he had originally picked up the rather unpleasant nickname 'Flapjack', but it certainly wasn't due to his good manners or friendly nature. He had burned all his bridges in Nocturne and most of the other major cities of Reverie some time ago, having sunk inevitably to the very bottom of the criminal underworld in each of them, one after the other.

As a result, Moonshine had been the only place left for him to try and carve out some sort of future. He had heard of its reputation as a haven for all sorts of strange individuals and troubled souls and sure enough, it had welcomed him with open arms a few weeks ago. Almost immediately he had found a place to live, somewhere that had met his two main (and only) criteria of being both cheap and available. Within two more days he had found a job that suited his abilities pretty well. A position working the night shift, providing security for a company that, despite only recently moving into the area, now seemed to be employing pretty much half the population of Moonshine. However, amongst all the apparent good luck, which should have set off mental alarm bells straight away, as life had taught him early on that his wasn't a charmed existence, the job had turned out to be a mistake, a really big one.

"It's not fair," his panicking mind shouted at him as he ran, as if that was any help. It wasn't his fault... it had just been a series of really bad coincidences. To have been on night shift tonight, to have failed to pay full attention to his route, to have taken a wrong turn, and to have seen.... His mind recoiled from the memory, much too terrible to dwell upon for even a moment. Instead it pulled him back to the present, despite desperately not wanting to be there either. As it did so he barged through the last door that led out the back of the building and onto the cobbled street. The cold of the night air hit him hard in the face, making his eyes water after the muggy atmosphere of the factory. He paused for a moment to see if he could hear any sound of pursuit in the corridor behind him, any footsteps. Breathing heavily he leant with his arm resting against the nearest wall, but there seemed to be nothing above the sound of his own rasping breath, just the empty darkness.

Allowing himself a brief exhalation of relief he started to walk away from the building, trying to look as calm and natural as he could manage. It was only then, as he walked just beyond the glow of the nearest lantern that he heard it. A gentle jingling noise just behind him, musical and cheery, sounding almost like

Christmas bells. He spun around, certain that there had been nothing behind him only the moment before, and for a very, very brief moment Flapjack Johnson cursed his run of bad luck one final time.

WELCOME TO MOONSHINE: CHAPTER 1

Grimble wiggled his toes and immediately winced in discomfort as a riot of pins and needles began to work its way angrily from the end of his foot to his heavily bandaged ankle. His left leg, the source of his current problems, was raised in front of him, with his foot resting on a pile of carefully stacked cushions, stubby blunt toes sticking out from the end of his dressing. Until he had tried moving, the whole arrangement had felt remarkably (and surprisingly) comfortable. As a result, every now and then he would let this feeling overrule his natural pessimism and try some slight movement, always with the same painful result. Letting the pain in his leg subside, he concentrated instead on the glow of warm sunlight on his face, enjoying the swell of wellbeing it brought with it, pulling his attention back away from the lingering injury.

For the last three weeks he had slowly been recuperating, splitting his time between a comfortable bed inside the little townhouse and an equally comfortable chair out in the small, paved garden area. He thought back to the clash that had caused his injury and shuddered slightly, still troubled by the memories that sprung unwanted to the forefront of his mind. The brief, tumultuous battle with the Nightmares had nearly cost him his leg, but to his surprise and secret gratitude, Lucid had come to his aid just in time, turning what could have been a fatal moment into one which was merely extremely uncomfortable.

He sighed heavily, owing Lucid was going to be nearly as painful as any of the physical injuries he had picked up ... and much, much more annoying. Still, he thought to himself, despite his insistence that he wanted to be left in peace to recover, Lucid had visited him every single day, loping in on his ridiculously long legs, placing his stupidly tall hat on the table and making idiotic, pointless small talk in his incredibly frustrating accent. At this thought Grimble stared back across the yard, through the open window, and at the clock slowly marking the passing of time on the kitchen wall. As he thought, there was still more than an hour until Lucid was expected to turn up again and he was getting increasingly impatient for the chance to be annoyed at him once again. Turning back to face the brick wall of the yard he shuffled down slightly in his seat to find a comfortable resting position and closed his eyes, deciding the best way to pass the time until Lucid's arrival was with a quick snooze.

He was just starting to doze off when he was disturbed by a noise from across the yard's wall. It was a high warbling laugh, sprinkled liberally throughout with individual notes of humour and warmth, a laugh that was completely infectious and impossible to hear without smiling. Not seeming to be aware of this fact, or if he was aware, simply not caring, rather than smiling Grimble's scowl deepened and he slouched down further in his seat.

There was a pause in the laughter, a moment of silence and then a loud and unexpected belching noise, reverberating around the yard so violently it shook Grimble's teeth. When this settled he could hear the laughter again, moving away into the distance. Then there was another pause, a sound which could only be described as something like a cat playing the drums while falling down the stairs, then more laughter and finally a series of strange parping noises. As the last set of sounds faded the odd cacophony moved too far away for Grimble to hear any more details. "Oh for goodness sake," Grimble muttered to himself miserably, any momentary relaxation or pleasure completely forgotten. "That's the last thing I need, on top of everything else, whatever is she doing here?"

BOOKS IN THIS SERIES

The Daydreamer Chronicles
Join Adam and his companions as they fight to save both worlds from the schemes of the Nightmares

Welcome To Moonshine

Being the hero of Reverie is turning out to be much, much harder work than Adam was expecting....

There is another side to the Great Dream, a city where all the strangest dreams come from... Moonshine.

Ruled over by a mad Queen and full of chaos and oddity, up until now it had been left alone by the rest of world, a destination for the lost, the lonely and the strange.

But now there is something very, very bad growing in the heart of Moonshine, and whether they like it or not Adam and his friends are going to have to get to the bottom of it. If they don't then strange dreams will be the least of their problems.

'Welcome to Moonshine' is the second book in the Daydreamer Chronicles series.

Where Dreams End

Finally, Adam has found where his mum could be hidden....

She is somewhere deep within the Dream World of Reverie, but getting to her won't be easy.

For a start she is somewhere far on the other side of the world, a place where no sane person would ever choose to go, the place the Nightmares come from. Even worse than that, the Queen of the Nightmares has her own plans in place, and Adam is caught right in the middle of her schemes.

Then there is the small matter of a war between Nightmare factions, an impossible voyage across the great sea of dreams and clashes with the most ancient beings in all of Reverie.

Fortunately for Adam he has the help of an even odder group of friends than usual, which in Reverie means very odd indeed. But even with the help of friendly dream beings, Nightmare freedom fighters and clockwork cyborgs, this time Adam is in real trouble, stuck in the place where dreams end.

'Where Dreams End' is the third book in the Daydreamer Chronicles series.

Frozen Dreams

Adam thought he had won. The Queen of the Nightmares defeated and Reverie made safe; but he was wrong and now the Dream World is in greater danger than ever, with enemies both old and new threatening him from every side.

The best chance of saving the Stairway of Dreams could lie within Adam's pendant, and the only person able to unlock those secrets lives deep in the icy homeland of the Drömer.

It's a cold and inhospitable wasteland, and the only thing Adam and his friends are guaranteed is a frosty reception. To make matters worse there is a mysterious new Daydreamer in Reverie and only time will tell if they're a friend or foe.

'Frozen Dreams' is the fourth book in the Daydreamer Chronicles.

Tales From Reverie: Maya

This is a Novella length tale, giving a brand new perspective on the events in the first three books, especially if you ever wondered whatever happened to Maya.

Something bad is coming...
All Maya wanted was a new life, far away from the barren plains of the west. Unfortunately for her what she got was something very different and now she works for the 'Five', the self-proclaimed protectors of Reverie.

There are rumours of a new Horror forming on the fringes of the Dreamworld, and what was supposed to be just another mission is already turning out to be much worse than Maya could ever have expected, with the future of the entire world hanging in the balance.

Before Adam's adventures in Reverie ever began there was another hero fighting to protect the world from Nightmares. See the events of the Daydreamer Chronicles unfold from a completely different perspective.

No Daydreams, no powers, but a whole lot of trouble.

Printed in Great Britain
by Amazon

60026468R00109